The three men who had been standing together the whole night watched as Clint approached Laura Linquist and said good-bye.

"When are we supposed to try for him?" one of them asked.

"I haven't got word yet," the leader said. "Don't worry, it'll be soon."

"Maybe they want him to get deep into the campaign first," the third man said.

"That's a possibility," the leader said.

"Who's gonna pull the trigger?" the second man asked.

"We'll see," the leader said. "It'll all be in the orders."

"He's leavin'," the second man said.

"Let him go," the leader said. "The time will come, don't worry."

THE GUNSMITH

374

DEADLY ELECTION

J. R. ROBERTS

JOVE BOOKS, NEW YORK

THE BERKLEY PUBLISHING GROUP
Published by the Penguin Group
Penguin Group (USA) Inc.
375 Hudson Street, New York, New York 10014, USA

Penguin Group (Canada), 90 Eglinton Avenue East, Suite 700, Toronto, Ontario M4P 2Y3, Canada
(a division of Pearson Penguin Canada Inc.) • Penguin Books Ltd., 80 Strand, London WC2R 0RL,
England • Penguin Group Ireland, 25 St. Stephen's Green, Dublin 2, Ireland (a division of Penguin
Books Ltd.) • Penguin Group (Australia), 707 Collins Street, Melbourne, Victoria 3008, Australia
(a division of Pearson Australia Group Pty. Ltd.) • Penguin Books India Pvt. Ltd., 11 Community
Centre, Panchsheel Park, New Delhi—110 017, India • Penguin Group (NZ), 67 Apollo Drive,
Rosedale, Auckland 0632, New Zealand (a division of Pearson New Zealand Ltd.) • Penguin Books
(South Africa) (Pty.) Ltd., Rosebank Office Park, 181 Jan Smuts Avenue, Parktown North 2193,
South Africa • Penguin China, B7 Jiaming Center, 27 East Third Ring Road North,
Chaoyang District, Beijing 100020, China

Penguin Books Ltd., Registered Offices: 80 Strand, London WC2R 0RL, England

This is a work of fiction. Names, characters, places, and incidents either are the product of the
author's imagination or are used fictitiously, and any resemblance to actual persons, living or
dead, business establishments, events, or locales is entirely coincidental.

DEADLY ELECTION

A Jove Book / published by arrangement with the author

PUBLISHING HISTORY
Jove edition / February 2013

Copyright © 2013 by Robert J. Randisi.
Cover illustration by Sergio Giovine.

ISBN: 978-0-515-15315-6

JOVE®
Jove Books are published by The Berkley Publishing Group,
a division of Penguin Group (USA) Inc.,
375 Hudson Street, New York, New York 10014.
JOVE® is a registered trademark of Penguin Group (USA) Inc.
The "J" design is a trademark of Penguin Group (USA) Inc.

PRINTED IN THE UNITED STATES OF AMERICA

10 9 8 7 6 5 4 3 2 1

ALWAYS LEARNING   **PEARSON**

ONE

Clint had been to Washington, D.C., recently, after a long absence. It was enough for him. That was the reason he refused to return again so soon even when he received the telegram asking for a meeting with a man named Jeremy Pike.

Pike was a Secret Service agent, a sometime partner to Clint's friend Jim West. This was the only reason Clint agreed to meet the man—not in Washington, D.C., itself, but in the West Virginia town of Meadowbrook.

Clint would have ridden Eclipse all the way, but Pike stressed the importance of their meeting, so he took the railroad. He got off the train at the station and took a horse-drawn cab to a hotel.

"Which one?" the driver asked.

"The nearest one," Clint said. "It doesn't really matter."

"Nearest one ain't so good, mister," the driver said. "You wouldn't thank me for takin' you there."

"Okay," Clint said, "take me to the nearest decent hotel."

"Yessir."

The driver took him to a small hotel called The Red Rooster Inn. There was a crude drawing of a red rooster over the door.

"Okay," the driver said, "we're here."

Clint paid the fare, stepped down with his carpetbag. He didn't have a rifle with him. His gun and holster were in the bag and his little Colt New Line was tucked into his belt, where nobody could see it, in the small of his back and covered by a jacket.

"You gonna need a driver to maybe look around town?" the young man asked.

"I don't think so," Clint said. "I think I'll only be here for one day."

"You're gonna wanna go someplace, though, right?"

"I'm supposed to go to a restaurant called O'Day's tonight."

"I know where that is," the man said. "Too far to walk. I'll pick ya up. What time?"

"Um, how far is it?"

"Twenty-minute ride."

"Four thirty would do, then." He was supposed to meet Pike at five.

"I'll be here," the young man said cheerfully, and drove off.

Clint checked in, took a look at his room, freshened up, and was in front of the hotel at four twenty-five when the young man pulled up.

"Told you I'd be here."

"And five minutes early," Clint said, climbing into the back of the cab. "I'm impressed."

The young man snapped the reins at his horse.

"How about I take the long route, give you a look at our town?" he asked.

"That's not necessary," Clint said. "I'm not going to be here that long."

"Okay, suit yourself."

He drove directly to the restaurant, pulled to a stop in front.

"Here ya go," he said.

It was four fifty, ten minutes early for his meet with Pike. But knowing Jeremy Pike—and he did, though not as well as he knew Jim West—he knew the man would be waiting inside.

He paid the kid and said, "Thanks."

"Want me to pick you up and take you back to your hotel?"

"Yes," Clint said. "Come back at seven."

"Sure you'll be done by then?"

"If I'm not," Clint said, "you can wait for me. I'll pay you."

"Okay," the driver said. "I'll see you then."

Clint turned and entered the restaurant. It was busy, most of the tables occupied. A man came up to him and asked, "Can I help you, sir?"

Just then Clint spotted Pike toward the back. The man saw him at the same time, and waved.

"I see my friend," Clint said.

The man turned, saw Pike waving, and said to Clint, "Very well. Enjoy your dinner, sir."

"Thank you."

He crossed the room, ducking between tables as he went. By the time he got there, Pike was on his feet with a big smile on his face. It had been a few years, and while Pike had a few more lines around his eyes and mouth, and a gray hair or two, he was still a natty dresser, with a quick, infectious smile.

"Clint," he said with his hand out, "great to see you."

"Jeremy." They shook hands.

"Jim sends his best."

Clint sat across from Pike, who reclaimed his seat.

"Where is he? Washington?"

"When is Jim ever in Washington?" Pike asked.

"You've got a point."

"He's actually out of the country now, on assignment. Thanks for coming so quickly."

"Your telegram said it was urgent."

"I would have met you halfway," Pike said, "but I'm on assignment myself, and have to stay close to Washington."

"This is fine."

Pike waved, and as if by magic, a waiter appeared with two steaming plates.

"I took the liberty of ordering steak dinners. They're very good here."

"Fine. I'm starving."

The waiter set the plates down in front of them.

"Coffee or beer?" Pike asked.

"Let's start with beer."

Pike nodded to the waiter.

"Can we talk while we eat?" Clint asked, picking up his knife and fork. "I'd like to find out what's on your mind."

"That's easy," Pike said. "I want you to run for Congress, Clint."

TWO

"You what?" Clint asked, his fork halfway to his mouth with a tantalizing hunk of steak on the end.

"Put that in your mouth before it falls off," Pike suggested.

Clint did, and chewed.

"It's very simple," Pike said. "Next month some men are going to come and see you, and they're going to ask you to run for Congress, to represent Texas in Washington, D.C."

"Why would they do a fool thing like that?" Clint asked. "I don't want to be a politician."

"I know that," Pike said, cutting up his own steak, "but we've been having some problems with our elections in this country."

"What kind of problems?"

"Well," Pike said, "to put it quite simply, somebody keeps killing the candidates."

"What?"

"Over the past eight years, eleven politicians who were running for office—specifically for Congress—have been killed."

"Why have I not heard about this before?"

"We kept it quiet," Pike said, "while we investigated."

"And what have you come up with?"

"Nothing."

"When did this last happen?"

"Two years ago."

"So let me get this straight," Clint said. "After being unable to find these killers over the past eight years you—your bosses—have decided to put somebody on the inside."

"That's correct."

"And you want it to be me?"

"After some discussion," Pike said, "yes."

"Even if I agree to this," Clint said, "what makes you think the killers will try for me?"

"They appear to target men who they know would make a difference," Pike said. "They're not often well-known men, which is why we've been able to keep it pretty quiet. But you, you're well known and you would make a difference. Clint, I think running for office would pretty much paint a target on your back."

"From what you've told me, I agree," Clint said.

"Then you agree to run?"

"That's not what I said," Clint replied. "I said I agree that would paint a target on me."

"Well, okay," Pike said, "we're agreed on that. What about running?"

"How can you be sure I'll be asked?" Clint asked. "Are you arranging that?"

"No," Pike said, shaking his head. "The offer will be legit, from the Democrats. You're not a Republican, are you?"

"I'm not affiliated with any political party," Clint said.

"Okay, good."

"Does the president know about this plan?" Clint asked.

"President Cleveland is behind the plan one hundred percent."

Clint ate some more steak, washed it down with a swig of beer.

"You need time to think about it," Pike said.

"Yes, I do."

"That's fine," Pike said. "Take all night."

"All night?" Clint asked. "You want an answer in the morning?"

"We're kind of getting down to the wire, Clint," Pike said. "Campaigns are about to start."

Clint jabbed his fork into his last piece of steak.

"Well?" Pike asked.

"I'll give it some thought overnight," Clint said.

"And answer in the morning?"

"If I can."

"I have to go back to Washington in the afternoon, Clint," Pike warned him.

"Look," Clint said, "how the hell can this work? I'm not a politician."

"It worked for Sam Houston," Pike said. "He was a senator and the governor of Texas. Go back even further than that. Davy Crockett was a congressman. Neither of them were politicians."

"I'm not in that company," Clint said.

"Don't be modest, Clint," Pike said. "You're every bit as legendary as both those men."

"You're nuts."

"Hey," Pike said, "remember, this wasn't my idea. We just caught wind of this and wanted to let you know."

"And you want me to agree to run," Clint said. "I don't want to be a congressman, Jeremy."

"Running doesn't mean you'll win," Pike said.

"You have a point there," Clint said, "but you do want somebody to try to kill me."

"Uh, technically that's correct."

"Well, Jeremy," Clint said, "I think you can see how that would cause me some concern."

"I would think you'd be concerned that somebody has been killing politicians for the past eight years."

Clint raised his eyebrows at his friend.

"Yeah okay," Pike said, "that didn't come out right. I know a lot of people feel that politicians deserve to die."

"No argument from me."

"But we can't just let it go on, Clint."

"Why doesn't Jim West run for office?"

"Nobody knows who he is," Pike said. "That's sort of the point of being in the Secret Service—accent on 'Secret.'"

"Yeah, yeah," Clint said, "I get it."

They both put down their utensils and the waiter took their plates away.

"Pie?" Jeremy asked.

"How often do I get the government to buy me dinner?" Clint asked. "You bet your ass, pie."

THREE

Pike and Clint walked outside together. The young driver was there waiting, sitting in his seat, staring off into space. When he saw Clint, he hurriedly dropped down to the ground.

"Can we give you a ride?" Clint asked.

"No, that's okay," Pike said. "I'll walk."

"Are you staying near here?"

Pike didn't answer, gave Clint an amused look.

"Okay, I get it," Clint said, "Accent on 'Secret.'"

Pike held his index finger to his lips and smiled.

"Where should I meet you tomorrow morning?" Clint asked.

"Let's have breakfast right here at eight a.m.," Pike suggested.

"Yeah, okay," Clint said. "Breakfast. I'll see you then."

He got into the back of the cab. By the time he turned to look, Pike was gone.

"Where to, mister?"

"Back to the hotel. What's your name?"

"Henry."

"I'm Clint," he said. "Back to my hotel, Henry."

"Gotcha."

In front of his hotel Clint paid the boy and said, "Pick me up tomorrow morning, seven thirty."

"That it for tonight?" Henry asked. "It's still early. Thought you might wanna find some excitement."

"Is there excitement in this town?"

"If you know where to look, there is."

Clint thought a moment, then said, "I don't think so. Thanks, Henry."

"Sure thing, Clint."

"Good night."

"Night."

Clint entered the lobby, which was empty except for the desk clerk, who was standing behind the desk, looking bored. He glanced over at Clint and smiled meekly. Clint returned the smile and went upstairs.

He sat on the bed and pulled off his boots. Running for Congress seemed like an insane idea to him. What were they supposed to do if he won? Of course, thinking that he could win was strange also. In fact, it was downright crazy.

He shook his head in wonder at the whole thing.

In the morning he woke, washed up, dressed, and packed his things. He had read Dickens for a few hours last night before turning in. This morning he awoke with his decision already made.

He went down to the lobby, told the clerk he'd be

checking out. He walked outside, found Henry waiting for him.

"Mornin', Clint," the young man said.

"Good morning, Henry."

He tossed his bag into the cab and climbed into the back. To this point there hadn't been a minute since he woke up that he questioned his decision. There was no point in second-guessing himself.

Henry drove him to the restaurant, where he found Pike waiting at the same table. The restaurant, as it had been the night before at dinnertime, was crowded at breakfast.

"I ordered steak and eggs," Pike said. "That okay?"

"That's fine."

The waiter poured coffee for both of them.

"Sleep well?" Pike asked.

"I slept great."

"So I gather you've come to a decision?"

"I have."

"And that is?"

"I'll do it," Clint said, "with one condition."

"What's that?"

"If I happen to win," Clint said, "I won't serve."

"Clint," Pike said, "believe me when I tell you nobody wants you in Congress."

"Well," Clint said, "doesn't that make me feel better about the whole thing."

"Okay," Pike said, "I didn't mean it to sound that way. What I meant was, we don't really want you to be a congressman. We just want you to find out who is killing our candidates."

"Who will my contact be in the government?"

"I will. You'll have several telegraph addresses where

you can reach me. One of them will get to me at a moment's notice."

"Who is going to approach me?"

"A delegation from Texas," Pike said. "I'm not sure who it will be, but I suspect there'll be someone from the governor's office, and there'll be someone with experience who will manage your campaign."

"My campaign," Clint said, shaking his head. "I never thought I'd hear those two words, let alone say them myself."

The waiter came with their breakfast and they sat back, fell silent while he served and left.

"How will they contact me?" Clint asked. "And where?"

"Just live your life, Clint," Pike said. "They'll find you."

"Probably in Labyrinth," Clint said. "I'll stay in Labyrinth for a while."

"That'll do."

They ate breakfast, talked about some of Pike's recent experiences, and then some of Clint's.

When they were done, they stopped outside and shook hands.

"Where to for you?" Clint asked.

"Back to Washington," Pike said. "Don't worry, you'll be able to get to me."

"Okay."

"The president is extremely pleased, Clint," Pike said. "He won't forget this."

"I'll make sure I call in the debt before he's out of office," Clint said.

Clint walked to Henry's cab and got in.

"Where to, boss?"

"The train station," Clint said.

FOUR

Pike had warned Clint that the time for campaigning was drawing near. With two weeks gone by, he was starting to wonder if the delegation had changed their minds.

Clint was in Labyrinth, at Rick's Place, having a drink with his friend Rick Hartman.

Upon his arrival in Labyrinth, he had sat down with Rick and told him the whole story . . .

"You're kiddin' me," Rick had said when Clint first explained the plan.

"I'm not."

"Congress?"

Clint nodded.

"Clint Adams, Congressman . . . I like it."

"I don't."

"Then why run?"

"There's more to it than that." He told him the rest, then sat back.

"You're painting a target on your back again," Rick said.

"I know."

"And for what? For nothin'? For no pay? Oh, wait, I know. For your country."

Clint stared at him.

"Okay," Rick said finally, "okay, never mind. You don't have to explain it to me. Hey, it might not even happen . . ."

Now, two weeks later, three men in suits walked into Rick's Place and looked around.

"Uh-oh," Rick said.

"I see them," Clint said.

"I think the delegation from the state capital just arrived."

"You want to be my campaign manager?" Clint asked.

"What?"

"One of them is planning to do it, but you could do it."

"Not me."

"Why not?"

"Because I'm not leavin' here and goin' to the capital," Rick said. "But I'll help you any other way I can . . . Congressman."

Rick had already gotten word that the lieutenant governor of the State of Texas had checked into the Labyrinth House Hotel earlier in the day.

"Here they come," Rick said. "I'll take my leave."

"Wait," Clint said, "I'll introduce you."

"That's okay," Rick said, standing up, "I'm not lookin' to add any politicians to my list of acquaintances. I'll see you later."

Rick slipped away as the three men reached Clint's table.

"Mr. Adams?" one of them asked.

"That's right."

"I certainly hope we didn't interrupt anything," the spokesman said. He was well dressed in a brown three-piece suit, holding a matching derby in his hands. He looked to be in his mid-thirties, had a pale complexion that indicated he did most of his work indoors. In fact, all the men had roughly the same look to them.

"Not at all," Clint said. "That was the owner, and he has work to do. What can I do for you gents?"

"Well, sir," the spokesman said proudly, "this gentleman is Thomas Benton Wheeler, the lieutenant governor of this great State of Texas." He indicated the oldest of the three, a man in his early fifties. When Clint showed no indication of being impressed, the man went on. "This is Walter Dixon, the chairman of the Democratic Party in Texas." This one was in his forties, had a rather amused look on his face. He didn't seem concerned that Clint wasn't impressed.

"And you, sir?"

"My name is William Gryder, although all my friends call me Will."

"Well, I don't know if we're friends or not, Mr. Gryder," Clint said. "Not until I know what's on your minds."

"May we sit down?"

"Please."

The lieutenant governor and Chairman Dixon sat down, but Gryder remained standing.

"Can I get anyone a drink?" he asked. "Mr. Adams? Another beer, on the State of Texas?"

"How can I turn that down?"

"Governor?"

"I assume they won't have a fine brandy," Wheeler said. "A beer will be fine."

Dixon simply nodded his agreement.

Oddly, the other two men did not speak while Gryder was getting the drinks. The man made two trips to and from the bar until he had set four beers down on the table, and then finally sat down.

"Mr. Adams," Gryder said, "we are here to make you a very interesting offer."

"What we hope will be a very interesting offer," Dixon added nervously.

"Yes, of course," Gryder said. He gave Dixon a look that was meant to say, "Quiet!"

The lieutenant governor took a sniff of his beer, made a face, tried a small sip, then made another face and put the beer down.

"Mr. Adams," Gryder said, "we all know your reputation. You are a true legend of the West."

"Thank you for not saying 'Old' West," Clint said.

"No, no," Gryder said, "we feel that you are very current, and just the man we need."

"Need for what?" Clint asked, playing dumb.

Gryder exchanged glances with the other two men. Dixon bit his lip, as if in an attempt to remain silent. The lieutenant governor simply shrugged.

"Clint," Gryder asked, "have you ever thought about running for public office?"

"You mean, like, for sheriff?" Clint asked. "I've been a sheriff. I don't want to do that again."

"No, no," Gryder said, "I'm talking about something bigger."

"Bigger?"

Gryder nodded.

"Clint, we'd like you to run for Congress."

Clint looked at the three men, all of whom were staring at him expectantly, and then said, "Are you kidding?"

FIVE

"We're quite serious," Gryder said.

"Here's a question," Clint said. "Why me?"

"Because you have a name," Gryder said, "and a reputation for being your own man. We think that's the kind of man people want in office now."

"But . . ." Clint said, playing his part, "I'm not a politician."

"Neither were Davy Crockett or Sam Houston, and look what they did," Gryder said.

It was not lost on Clint that this was the same argument Jeremy Pike had used.

"Who's this coming from?" Clint asked. "The president?"

"Hardly," Wheeler said, speaking for the first time. "President Cleveland hardly cares who runs for office in Texas."

Clint thought back to what Pike had said about the president endorsing the plan. Undoubtedly Washington and the Secret Service were involved in ways these men were not aware of.

He waited for Wheeler to continue, but the lieutenant governor seemed to have said what he wanted to say. He left it to Gryder to go on.

"Governor Ross was the one who came up with your name, Clint," Gryder said.

"The governor, huh?" Clint said. "Guess I should be flattered."

"You'll have a campaign staff, headed up by me," Gryder said.

"I assume you've done this before?"

"Many times."

"Successfully?"

"I've won more than I've lost," Gryder said.

"I see."

The three men were staring at Clint again.

"So what do you think?" Gryder asked. "How's it sound?"

"I'm not sure," Clint said. "I'll have to know a little bit more."

"I can tell you more," Gryder said. "Why don't we have dinner tonight and talk some more?"

"Okay," Clint said. "What hotel are you at?"

"The Labyrinth House."

"They have a great dining room," Clint said. "Let's eat there."

"That'll be fine."

The three men stood up.

"Just the two of us," Clint added.

"I beg your pardon?" Wheeler asked.

"No offense, Mr. Wheeler," Clint said, "but I think my campaign manager and I should speak alone."

Wheeler and Dixon exchanged a glance.

"Any objection?" Clint asked.

"No," Dixon said, "no objection."

"None," Wheeler said.

"Good," Clint said. "Then I'll see you at seven, Mr. Gryder."

"Seven it is."

The three men left the place. As they did, Rick came walking back over and sat down.

"Gave them kind of a hard time, didn't you?" he asked. "I mean, you knew they were comin' and why."

"I didn't want to give in too fast," Clint said. "Let them work for it."

"They tell you what party they want you to run with?" Rick asked.

"The Democrats. After all, the governor is a Democrat."

"Yeah, he is," Rick said. "And so's the president." He waited a beat, then said, "I didn't vote for either of them."

SIX

The three men from the state capital walked back to their hotel, and stopped in the lobby.

"What do you think?" Wheeler asked.

"I don't know," Dixon said.

"He'll do it," Gryder said.

"What makes you think so?" Wheeler asked.

"Why would he not?" Gryder asked. "We're talking about power, prestige . . . and money."

"You think everyone wants that?" Dixon asked.

"Everyone should," Wheeler said. "If he doesn't, he's a fool."

"I'm not sure about this," Dixon said.

"You haven't been sure from the start, Dix," Gryder said.

"He's a gunfighter," Dixon said, "not a politician."

"Do I have to make the Crockett and Houston arguments with you?" Gryder asked.

"Clint Adams is no Sam Houston," Dixon said.

"Maybe not," Gryder said. "But all we need him to be is Clint Adams."

"I'm going to my room," the lieutenant governor said. "Let me know what happens tonight."

"Yes, sir."

They both watched Wheeler walk up the steps.

"Why'd he have to come along?" Gryder asked.

"He's representing the governor," Dixon said.

"You could've done that, Dix."

"Me? I don't want to represent the governor. I represent the party. That's enough for one man."

"Yeah, I guess."

"You really think he's gonna run, Will?"

"I think he will."

"For the power, or the prestige? Maybe the money?"

"None of the three, I'll bet."

"Then why?"

Gryder shrugged.

"Maybe just to be able to do something for his country."

"Patriotism?" Dixon asked with a laugh.

"Why not?"

"That's a lot to expect these days, Will," Dixon said. "I thought you were a lot more realistic than that."

"You mean cynical, don't you?"

"Yeah, well, that, too."

"Maybe I am," Gryder said, "or was. But do you know who we just finished talking to over at that saloon? The goddamn Gunsmith."

"Don't tell me you're impressed?"

"Come on, Dix," Gryder said. "What we just did was like meeting Wild Bill Hickok."

"Hickok's dead."

"But he's a legend."

"He was a backshooter."

"I know he was shot in the back," Gryder said. "I don't know that he was a backshooter, too."

"Come on, Will," Dixon said. "Don't go changin' on me now. Don't leave me out here all alone."

Gryder put his hand on Dixon's shoulder.

"You're not alone, Dix," Gryder said. "Don't worry."

"What about Carla?"

"What about her?"

"Are we gonna use her?"

Gryder thought for a moment, then said, "I'll take her to dinner tonight with me."

"He said for you to come alone."

"He wants me to come without the two of you," Gryder said. "When he sees Carla, I don't think he'll object, do you?"

Dixon said, "What man would?"

SEVEN

Clint appeared in the lobby of the Labyrinth House Hotel at 6:55 p.m. People were coming and going from the dining room, in both couples and groups. He stepped to the entrance to look inside, saw Will Gryder sitting at a table with a beautiful, black-haired woman. At least he'd left the other two politicians behind. Clint wondered if this woman was meant to be added incentive for him to run. If she was, he could see where it might work.

He entered the dining room, walked across the floor to the table, and looked down at Gryder, who looked up at him in surprise.

"There you are!"

"Weren't you expecting me?"

"Well, yes, of course." Gryder jumped to his feet. "Clint, I'd like you to meet Carla Beckett. Carla, this is Clint Adams."

"Mr. Adams," she said, "I'm happy to meet you."

"Miss Beckett."

"Oh, Carla, please," she said, "especially if we're going to be working together."

"Are we?" Clint asked.

"Carla will be working on your campaign," Gryder said. "That is, if you agree to run. Please, sit down. Let's have some breakfast."

Clint sat across from Carla, to Gryder's left. A waiter came over and poured him some coffee.

"Have you ordered?" Clint asked.

"Not until you got here," Gryder said.

"That would not have been polite," Carla said. "What's good, Mr. Adams?"

"Everything," he said. "They have a real good kitchen here. And please, call me Clint . . . Carla."

Both Carla and Gryder ordered Spanish omelets, while Clint ordered his usual steak and eggs.

"So, what exactly would you be doing during the campaign?" Clint asked Carla.

"Mainly," she said as he sipped his coffee, "keeping you happy . . ."

He choked.

"And on time."

"Carla would pretty much be your secretary—"

"Assistant," she corrected.

"And would accompany you to most functions."

"What kinds of functions?"

"Mostly rallies, and fund-raisers."

The waiter came with their breakfast and set the plates in front of them.

"Maybe," Clint said, "while we eat, you and Carla can tell me exactly what I'd be in for."

"We can do that," Gryder said. "Carla, why don't you start . . ."

Clint noticed how Gryder allowed Carla to do most of the talking. She was as smart as she was beautiful. And she made her points very well—although after listening, Clint still wondered why anyone would ever want to be a politician.

Clint finished the last piece of his steak and pushed his plate away. Gryder had finished his breakfast, while Carla had eaten only half.

"So, Clint," Gryder asked, "what do you think?"

"Where are your cohorts?" Clint asked.

"Probably in their rooms," Gryder said. "And after today they might be your cohorts as well. That is, if you agree to run."

"I'd have to move to Austin, right?"

"Well, yeah . . . it is the capital, Clint."

"Where would I live?"

"We'll have a house for you."

"A house?"

"Of course," Gryder said. "And you'll have a staff."

"A staff? You mean, like Carla?"

"No, I mean at home," Gryder said. "You'll have a butler, and a cook."

"Jesus."

"And the state will pay for it all," Carla reminded him.

"True, but . . ."

"Don't worry, Clint," Gryder said. "We'll have it all set up."

"Wouldn't a hotel room be good enough?"

"Well, there's really no point in discussing it," Gryder said, "unless you agree to run."

"True."

"So what's your decision, Clint?" Carla asked.

"Well . . ." Clint said. "I guess we might as well give it a go."

"That's great!" Gryder said with relief.

"In my first act as your assistant," Carla said to Clint, "I think this calls for champagne."

EIGHT

After a champagne dessert Clint returned to Rick's Place. His friend was waiting to hear how his meeting went.

Clint got two beers at the busy bar and joined Rick at his table in the back of the room.

"How did it go?"

"Great meal," Clint said.

"You know what I mean. Did you give them the word?"

"I gave them the word."

"So when do you move to Austin?"

"Everything is time sensitive now, so they want me to go back with them tomorrow."

"You'll have to get a place to live."

"They're going to take care of that for me," Clint said. "They want me to have a house with a staff, but I'm trying to get them to put me in a hotel."

"A staff?"

"A butler, and a cook."

"Take it, Clint. Take whatever you can get. Make this job worth it."

"Yeah, but . . . servants? And I have an assistant."

"What's he like?"

"It's a she," Clint said. "Her name is Carla and she's beautiful."

"Are you sure she's an assistant?" Rick asked. "Maybe she's a high-priced whore."

"I thought about that," Clint said, "but she seems pretty smart."

"Whores are smart—some of them anyway."

"Well, she sounds intelligent about politics, and about society in Austin."

"Society," Rick said, making a face. "I hate those types."

"I'm definitely going to have to deal with them," Clint said. "Society and politics go hand in hand."

"Just don't shoot any of them."

"I'll try not to."

"Oh, hell," Rick said.

"What?"

"I just thought of something."

"What?"

"Am I gonna have to vote for you?"

"I don't think it's going to go that far."

"I hope not."

"What would be so bad about having me as a congressman?" Clint asked.

"Look, don't take this personally," Rick said, "but I vote Republican."

Clint shook his head at his friend. He didn't understand how anyone could do anything but vote for a man, not blindly for a party.

"When are you leaving?" Rick asked.

"Early stage tomorrow."

"Taking Eclipse with you?"

"No," Clint said, "I don't think he'd like a political campaign very much. Will you look after him for me?"

"Of course I will," Rick said, "and I gotta wish you luck."

"I'm not really running, Rick," Clint said. "I mean, even if I win, I'm not going to serve."

"Not what I meant," Rick said. "I'm talking about once again painting a bull's-eye on your back."

"Oh, that."

"Who's gonna watch your back?"

"Well," Clint said, "since I'll be in Texas for a while, I do have an idea about that."

"Oh?" Rick said. "Anything you'd like to share?"

"Not right now," Clint said. He stood up. "I've got to pack."

"Why?" Rick asked. "I'm sure they're also going to buy you new clothes when you get to Austin."

He was right. They had already told Clint that Carla would be taking him shopping for an entire new wardrobe.

"I'll keep in touch," Clint said.

"You better," Rick said. "I've got to hear how this one goes."

NINE

Upon arrival in Austin, Clint was taken by Gryder and Carla from the train station to his new house.

"Jesus," Clint said, looking at the white columns in front. It was two stories, looked like many homes Clint had seen in the South. "I guess you couldn't get me into a hotel."

"We could still do that," Gryder said, "but why don't you just give this a try? See how it feels?"

"Come on," Carla said, taking hold of Clint's arm, "let's take a look."

They walked up the front steps to the door and Gryder knocked. A man in a black suit and tie opened the door, stared at them without expression.

"Mr. Gryder," he said. "How nice to see you. And Miss Beckett."

"Hello, Julius," Carla said. "I want you to meet Mr. Clint Adams."

"The candidate," Gryder added.

"Julius," Clint said, extending his hand, "nice to meet you."

"It wouldn't be seemly for the butler to shake hands with the master, sir," Julius said, "but it's my pleasure to meet you."

He opened the large white door for the three of them to enter.

"Is Mrs. Bigelow here?" Carla asked.

"Yes, miss, she's in the kitchen."

"Good, we want her to meet Mr. Adams as well."

"I will tell her to make herself available, miss."

"Thank you."

"Look," Clint started, "I don't know about this—"

"Let me show you the rest of the house," Carla said, rubbing his arm and pressing her hip against his.

"I'll see about dinner," Gryder said. "See you two a little later."

Carla tugged Clint over to the stairway and said, "Why don't we start upstairs?"

Clint allowed himself to be led upstairs, but knew he was going to have to put a stop to this. He couldn't let Carla think she could get away with using her wiles to lead him around for the length of the campaign.

Upstairs she showed him several bedrooms before taking him to the largest one.

"This is the master bedroom," she said, "your bedroom."

She released his arm, walked to the huge, oversized bed, and sat down on it. She was wearing a comfortable, loose-fitting dress which had been meant for comfort on the train. Her jet-black hair was up, revealing her long, beautiful, pale neck. She studied him and licked her full lower lip.

"What do you think?" she asked.

"I think we need to make some rules."

"What kind of rules?" She tilted her head to the left, used the fingers of her right hand to gently touch her neck.

"You have to stop thinking you can lead me around by the nose, Carla."

"The nose, Clint?" she asked, smiling. "I haven't been leading you around by the . . . nose."

His cock was hard, and it would have been easy for him to take her right there on that big bed—but that was what she wanted. That would have meant she was still in control.

"You and I will get along," he told her, "as soon as you realize who the boss is. Now come on, let's go downstairs and have something to eat. I need to get cleaned up . . . and so do you."

"But—" she said, but before she could get any further, he turned and walked out.

Cleaned up? she thought. She sniffed herself, then called out, "Hey, wait," and ran after Clint.

TEN

Clint was shown to a room with indoor plumbing where he could clean up. He was told there was another such room right off his master bedroom. Carla had not shown that to him.

When he'd finished, Carla went in and used the facilities, and then Gryder got himself cleaned up as well. They then all met in the dining room, where the butler, Julius, was waiting.

"Sir?" he said to Clint, holding out the chair at the head of the long, mahogany table.

Clint decided to go ahead and sit there. He'd put his foot down about this stuff later.

Gryder sat to his right, and Carla on his left. She was still stinging because of her failed attempt to seduce Clint and completely wrap him around her finger. Clint had guessed what she was up to when Gryder said to them, "See you a little later."

Now she knew he wouldn't tumble into bed with her when she crooked her finger. He wondered if she would tell Gryder that he'd walked out on her.

The door to the kitchen opened and a middle-aged woman came out, carrying plates.

"Clint, this is Mrs. Bigelow," Gryder said.

"Mrs. Bigelow," he said. He didn't offer to shake hands, not because it would be unseemly, but because her hands were full.

She set the plates down in front of them, glared at them, and then returned to the kitchen.

"What's wrong with her?" Clint asked.

"My fault," Gryder said. "I telegraphed ahead and told her to make a simple dinner. She wanted to welcome you with a proper four-course meal."

Clint looked down at the steak and potatoes she had set before them.

"This looks great."

"Yes, in my telegram I told her that you liked steak."

There was some noise from another part of the house and Clint noticed that Julius was gone.

"Where's Julius?"

"He's having your things brought up to your room," Gryder said. "Tomorrow, Carla will take you shopping for your wardrobe. And tomorrow night will be your first function."

"Function?"

"That's what they call them," Carla said. "It's actually a party."

"Ah, a party," Clint said. "I see. Well, why don't we eat these steaks before they get cold."

They each attacked their dinners.

* * *

When they were finished, Mrs. Bigelow came in and collected the plates.

"That was excellent, Mrs. Bigelow," Clint said. "I can't remember when I had a better steak."

She hesitated, then the grim set of her face cracked slightly.

"Thank you, sir. Will you be wanting dessert? I prepared a peach pie."

"Peach?"

"Yes sir," she said. "I was told it was your favorite."

"Yes, it is. I'd love peach pie."

"And coffee?"

"Yes, thank you."

"Black, and strong?"

"Exactly."

"Coming up."

She left the dining room and Clint looked at Gryder.

"You have me well scouted, Mr. Gryder."

"Will, please."

"All right, Will."

"Yes, sir," Gryder said. "You see, that's my job. To make sure everything is right."

"I thought that was Carla's job."

"Um, yes, well," Gryder said, "it's her job, too."

"Tell me who I'll be meeting at this party tomorrow night."

"Local dignitaries," he said, "and possible contributors to your campaign."

"Ah, the contributors."

"They're necessary," Gryder said, "if we're to run a strong campaign."

"I suppose so."

Mrs. Bigelow came out and put a slice of pie before each of them. Clint noticed that his was twice the size of anyone else's. She then walked around and poured coffee for them all.

"Anything else, sir?" she asked.

"Wait," Clint said.

She stood there while he took a chunk out of the pie and tasted it.

"Oh, my God," he said, "this is the best peach pie I've ever had."

This time she almost smiled.

"Perhaps," she said, "tomorrow night I'll be able to cook you a proper meal."

"We won't be here for dinner tomorrow night, Mrs. Bigelow," Gryder said.

"We have a party to attend," Carla said.

Mrs. Bigelow sighed.

"What about breakfast?" Clint asked.

"Sir?"

"In the morning," he said, "I'd like a nice big breakfast."

"That would be fine, sir," she said. "Yes, that would be no problem."

"That's great."

She looked pointedly at his guests, whom she obviously had no use for, and asked, "Will there be any others for breakfast?"

"Yes," Gryder said, "Carla and I will both be here early."

"Very well," she said. "Three for breakfast. I'll see to it."

"Thank you, Mrs. Bigelow."

"I'll be in to clean up when you've finished your dessert."

She went back to the kitchen.

"She likes you," Gryder said.

"Does she?"

"And she absolutely hates us," Carla said.

"That's okay," Gryder said. "Clint's the one she'll be working for."

"About that—"

"If not," Gryder said, "if you should decide you prefer a hotel, well . . . Julius and Mrs. Bigelow will be let go."

"Let go?" Clint asked. "You mean . . . fired?"

"Well, yes," Gryder said, "I mean, if that's what you really want."

Clint thought about the steak that had almost melted in his mouth, and about the hunk of delicious peach pie before him. He picked up the cup of coffee and sipped it. It tasted wonderful.

That decided the matter.

"No, no," he said, cutting another hunk of pie and lifting it with his fork, "this house will be fine, just fine."

ELEVEN

Clint spent the night in a bed more comfortable than any he'd ever slept in before. In the morning, as the sun was streaming through the window, he didn't want to get up.

A man could get used to a bed like this—too used to it. He made himself rise.

He could smell the scent of breakfast coming from the kitchen, and decided to go down and surprise Mrs. Bigelow.

He walked through the dining room to the kitchen door. He knew he was taking a chance. Cooks in these kinds of houses were usually very territorial about their kitchens. He took a deep breath and walked in.

The sounds of bacon sizzling in a pan greeted him. Mrs. Bigelow turned to face him, a stern look on her face, but when she saw that it was him, her look softened.

"Good morning, sir," she said.

"Mrs. Bigelow," Clint said, "I'm not going to have any of that."

"Of what, sir?" she asked. "I don't understand."

"I want you to call me Clint, not sir."

"Oh, but I couldn't—"

"I'm going to have enough trouble with Julius," Clint said. "He's such a stuffed shirt, but you . . . I sense that you and I are going to be good friends."

She stood there with a spatula in her hand, and it could have gone one of two ways. She could have chased him from the kitchen, swinging it, or she could do what she did—smile.

"All right . . . Clint. If I give you a cup of coffee, will you get out of my kitchen?"

"I will," he said.

She poured him a cup and handed it to him, then smiled again as he backed out.

When he got out to the dining room, he heard a knock at the front door. He started to go to answer it, but saw Julius getting there ahead of him. He figured he might as well let the man do his job.

He stood back and watched as Julius opened the door, spoke, and then stepped back to allow the visitors to enter.

Carla came in first, followed by Will Gryder.

"Is Mr. Adams up yet?" Gryder asked.

"I believe he is in the kitchen with Mrs. Bigelow, sir."

"Really?" Gryder seemed surprised. "That lady doesn't usually let anybody into her kitchen."

"Nevertheless . . ." Julius said.

The fact that Julius knew Clint was in the kitchen led

Gryder to believe that the man pretty much knew everything that went on in the house.

Clint came walking out of the dining room with his coffee cup.

"Good morning," he called out.

Carla and Gryder looked his way.

Julius turned to face him and asked, "Is there anything I can do, sir?"

"Not right now, Julius," Clint said. "Have you had your breakfast?"

"I have, sir."

"Then you can go . . . and do whatever it is you . . . do about now."

"Yes, sir," Julius said with a bow. "Thank you, sir."

He walked away.

"Wow," Carla said, "the house smells great."

"Bacon," Gryder said.

"And much more," Clint said. "Come into the dining room."

He led them to the table, and as they sat, he stuck his head in the kitchen and said, "Mrs. Bigelow, our guests are here."

"Yes, si—Clint. I'll bring out some coffee."

"Thank you."

He turned to his guests and said, "Have a seat."

They took the same seats they'd had the night before.

"How'd you sleep, Clint?" Gryder asked.

"Like a log," Clint said. "Best night's sleep I've had in a long time, and the best bed I've ever been in."

"That's great," Gryder said. "I wanted to brief you a bit on the people you'll be meeting tonight. We can do that over breakfast, and then I'll turn you over to Carla. She's going to dress you."

"Dress me?"

"From head to toe," Gryder said.

"Will I have any say in what I wear?"

"Well, of course," Gryder said. "You'll have a say in everything. But just remember, we *are* the experts."

"We're all experts in one thing or another, Will," Clint said.

"That's true," Carla said.

Mrs. Bigelow came out of the kitchen with two cups of coffee and set them before Gryder and Carla.

"Thank you, Mrs. Bigelow," Gryder said.

She went back to the kitchen without speaking.

"How are you getting along with your cook?"

"Great," Clint said. "We have an understanding."

"That's good," Gryder said. "She's not an easy woman to get along with."

"Really?" Clint said. "I haven't found that."

Carla sipped her coffee and watched them.

"Well," Gryder said, "let me tell you a little about the people you'll be meeting tonight. Of course, the governor will be there . . ."

Gryder talked about the governor and other local dignitaries until Mrs. Bigelow came out carrying various plates. By the time she was done, the table was covered with eggs, bacon, potatoes, flapjacks, biscuits, and muffins, with their choice of honey or butter, and then maple syrup.

"It all looks great, Mrs. Bigelow."

"I hope you and your guests enjoy it, Clint."

As she went back to the kitchen, Gryder looked at him and said, "Clint?"

"Like I said," Clint replied, "we have an understanding."

"I guess so," Gryder said. "I don't know anyone else Mrs. Bigelow has ever had an understanding with."

"What can I say?" Clint asked. "I have a way with women."

"Some women," Carla said into her cup.

"I think we better eat while it's hot," Clint said, ignoring her. "Keep talking, Will."

They all reached for food while Gryder went on . . .

TWELVE

After breakfast Clint, Gryder, and Carla went into the living room so Gryder could finish his rundown on who Clint would be meeting that night.

"You'll have to be cordial and charming to everyone," Gryder ended. "After all, we need their money."

"Charm the women," Carla said.

Both men looked at her.

"Sorry?" Clint asked.

"Charm the women," she said again. "They'll get their husbands to give you money."

"She has a point," Gryder said. "The way to the men is through their women."

"What if they get jealous?"

"We said charm them," Gryder said, "not take them to bed."

"Will!" Carla said, but there was no blush. She was not as outraged as she wanted them to think.

"Well, all right," Clint said. "I guess I better get dressed for my little shopping trip with Carla."

"I'll be going," Gryder said. "Carla will pick you up tonight and bring you to the party."

"Where is it?"

"In the home of one of our biggest supporters."

"*Our* supporters?"

"Supporters of the party," Gryder said. "But after tonight I'm sure she will be yours as well."

As Gryder left, Clint looked at Carla and said, "She?"

"Many of the biggest contributors are women," she said. "Why don't you get dressed while I see if Mrs. Bigelow will give me some more coffee."

"I'll be down quick," Clint promised.

He went upstairs and put on a clean pair of jeans and a chambray shirt. He pulled his boots on, knowing that one thing Carla was probably going to insist on was new ones. He'd had these for months and they were just starting to fit well.

Last he grabbed his New Line, tucked it into the back of his shirt, then covered that with a lightweight jacket. When he came back down, Carla was standing in the front hall, drinking coffee and waiting.

"Is that shirt chambray?" she asked.

"It is," he said. "I picked it up in Labyrinth before we left."

She approached him, put her hand against his chest to feel the material.

"Maybe I don't have as much work to do as I thought." Then she looked down at his boots. "Or maybe I do."

"Shall we go?" Clint asked.

THIRTEEN

Clint was used to picking up his clothes from a general store or mercantile. Sometimes, when he was in San Francisco or New York, he'd buy something from one of the large men's clothing stores. The stores in Austin that Carla took him to were on par with those. Dedicated specifically to men's clothing, with tailors right there on staff to get the proper measurements.

Carla bought him shirts at first, then had him measured for some special suits.

"And we need one for tonight," she told the tailor.

"Tonight?"

"Yes," she said, "it's very important."

"It's very unusual," he said. "Not easy to make a suit in a matter of hours."

"Might you have something you already started for someone?" she asked. "Maybe they didn't pick it up?"

The tailor, a small man in his sixties, peered at her over the wire frame of his glasses.

"Yes, yes," he said, "I do have some unfinished suits. Wait, perhaps I have something that can be sized."

As the tailor went into a back room, Clint said, "I never would have thought to ask him that."

"That's why you have me," she said with a smile . . .

The tailor returned with a suit he said he thought would work. Clint tried it on. It had been made for a man larger in the shoulders and the waist.

"I can fix this," the tailor said, "and this . . . do you like the color?"

"It's blue," Carla said. "You can't go wrong with blue."

The tailor looked at Clint.

"Like the lady says," he replied, "blue's fine."

"Very well, then," the tailor said. "Let's just try on the vest . . ."

Clint put the vest on and the tailor made the necessary chalk marks for adjustment.

"When can this be ready?" Carla asked.

"Well, I close at five . . . four thirty?"

"That's wonderful," she said. "I'll pay for that one when we come back, and then pay for the others when we pick them up."

"Very well."

"Thank you so much."

They left the tailor carrying bundles of Clint's new shirts wrapped in brown paper.

"Where to now?" he asked.

"New boots," she said.

"How about lunch first?"

"Well," she said, "I am rather hungry, now that you

mention it. There's a small place just around the corner."

"Lead the way, ma'am."

They were getting along fine. She seemed to have forgotten the snub of the night before, and he was letting her attempts to control him go. When it came to the clothes, she did have more experience than he did, and she had good taste.

It seemed as if they were going to get along . . .

When Gryder left the house, he did not go back to his office. Neither did he go to see the lieutenant governor, or the governor. He would be seeing them later.

He went to another house, this one across town. It was small, well cared for, spread out on one level. Not as opulent as the house Clint Adams was in, it was nevertheless worth a lot of money, and was owned by a wealthy man.

Gryder went to the front door, looked around to see who was on the street, then knocked on the door. It was opened by a tall, impeccably dressed man in his fifties.

"Will," he said. "I've been waiting for you."

"Yes, I'm sorry," Gryder said. "I've been busy."

"With Mr. Adams?"

"Yes."

"And how is that going?"

"Fine, fine."

"Come in, then," the man said. "We have much to discuss."

"Yes, we do."

Gryder went inside, and the man closed the door.

"How has he taken to Carla?" the man asked.

"He's . . . resisting."

"Really?" the man said as they walked down a hall. "Given his reputation, I didn't think that would be possible."

"Don't worry," Gryder said. "He won't be able to resist for long."

"She is a lovely woman. Ah, here we are."

He led Gryder into a den, a room lined with books. The other three men there looked up from the books they had each been perusing.

"Ah," one of them said, "and here we are."

"Will is here to fill us in, gentleman," the host said. "But first, who wants a drink?"

FOURTEEN

Carla took Clint to a small café that had tables inside as well as outside. Carla wanted to sit outside, but Clint said no.

"Why not?"

"It's not very healthy for me to just . . . sit in plain sight."

"Oh, yes," she said, "I forgot. Your reputation. Someone might . . . shoot at you?"

"Someone might," he said, "but I'm more concerned that some innocent people might get caught in the cross fire."

"So your concern is for others?" she asked.

"Yes."

"That's very noble," she said. "Not something you would usually find in a politician."

"I'm not a politician."

They went inside and were shown to a table in the center of the room.

"How about one in the back?" Clint asked the waiter.

"Of course, of course," the man said. "Whatever you like."

He walked them to a table against the back wall, then handed them each a menu.

"Can I get you something to drink?" he asked.

"Hot tea for me," Carla said.

"Coffee," Clint said, "strong, and black."

"Yessir."

Carla had set the menu aside.

"Why don't you order for both of us?"

She smiled at him.

"You won't think I'm trying to control you?"

"No," he said, "I'll think that you're trying to get me a good meal."

"All right, then."

The waiter returned with their coffee and tea. Carla ordered a chicken platter for each of them, without referring to the menu.

"You can have a steak again tonight if you want," she reasoned.

"That's fine," he said. "I like chicken."

"Good."

While they waited, she asked him questions about himself, his past, some of which he answered, and some he didn't.

"You're not answering any of my questions that would give me insight into who you are," she said. "You're just telling me . . . stories."

"Why do you need insight?" he asked. "Would that help you figure out how to control me?"

"I thought we'd gotten past that."

"As far as lunch was concerned, yes."

"Look," she said, "I admit, yesterday I was . . . trying to seduce you."

"No fooling."

"It's part of my job."

"You mean . . ."

"No, I'm not a whore," she said. "Not exactly. It's just a way to keep you . . . happy."

"I can find my own women to keep me happy, thanks," Clint said. "Besides, I'm here to run for office, not find a bedmate."

"Fine," she said with a shrug. "Have it your way."

"If I was going to have it my way, I'd probably not even be here."

"So then why did you agree?"

"It's hard to explain."

"Because you were called?"

"I was drafted."

"Conscripted."

"Exactly."

"So you don't feel you could have said no?"

"I suppose it was an option," he said, wondering if he could tell her what she wanted to hear, "but if certain people who know what they're doing think that I'm the man for the job . . ."

He stopped as the waiter appeared with their meals. She had ordered herself a quarter of a chicken, while ordering him half, both meals broiled to perfection, with vegetables added.

Clint cut a piece off the breast and put it in his mouth. The skin was crisp and flavorful.

"How is it?" she asked.

"Great," he said, "but I'll bet Mrs. Bigelow could do better."

"I'm sure she could."

They proceeded to eat.

While they ate, they talked, and Clint realized he wasn't getting any more out of Carla than she had gotten from him about who she really was.

She had been born back East—as he had—and had come to the West to find a new life for herself when she was in her twenties. He had come even younger than that. Now she was in her early thirties, and had been living in Austin for the past five years, working for politicians.

But who she really was, and how she felt? He didn't have a clue.

"Come on," she said when they were finished, "let's go and look at some boots."

She took Clint to one of the best bootmakers in Austin. He sat and let the man fit him, tried on some ready-made boots before they decided he needed a custom-made pair.

"By tonight?" she asked.

"You're crazy," the bootmaker said.

"Well, we need a pair he can wear tonight."

So they continued to try on boots until they found a pair that fit.

Almost.

FIFTEEN

Clint's feet were hurting in his new boots, and his jacket—which had originally been cut for a larger man but had been taken in according to the current style—was tight across the shoulders.

He walked into the home of his hostess with Carla on his arm. She was lovely in a magenta gown that left her shoulders bare, showing the upper slopes of her generous breasts.

Clint was also wearing his gun and holster. Carla told him that Gryder wanted him to wear it.

"He says we want people to know who they're voting for," she'd said.

"That's fine with me," he'd said. "I'd rather wear it than not wear it."

The room they were in was the size of a ballroom. It was filled with people, and at the far end were a group of musicians, playing loudly. Gryder greeted Clint as he entered and said, "The governor wants to meet you."

"What about my hostess?" Clint asked.

"I think the governor comes first, Clint."

"Is he going to be contributing to my campaign fund?" Clint asked.

"Of course not," Gryder said. "He can't be caught doing—"

"Then I think my hostess should be first."

Gryder stared at Clint for a few moments, then shrugged and said, "Okay, if that's the way you want it. Come with me."

He led Clint and Carla across the room where a tall woman in a blue dress, much like the one Carla was wearing, was talking to several men who were staring at her cleavage.

"Excuse me, gentlemen," Gryder said. "Mrs. Linquist, this is our candidate, Clint Adams."

The woman turned to face Clint. She had creamy skin and a full, womanly body, but up close he could see she was about ten years older than Carla.

"Well, Mr. Adams," she said, extending her bejeweled hand. "This is a pleasure."

"The pleasure is mine, Mrs. Linquist," he said. "May I present Miss Carla—"

"Yes, yes, charmed, my dear," the woman said, dismissing Carla. She never took her eyes off Clint. While Carla had hold of his right arm, Mrs. Linquist moved in and claimed the left.

"I'd like to take you to meet my husband," she said, tugging on him.

"That'd be fine, ma'am," Clint said. "Where is he?"

"My husband is in a wheelchair, Mr. Adams—may I call you Clint?"

"Of course."

"And will you call me Laura?"

"If you like."

She tugged on his arm again, and Clint felt Carla's hold on his other arm strengthen. However, Gryder moved in and pried Carla off Clint's arm, so that Laura Linquist could pull him along.

"I'd like it very much," she said, pressing her breasts to his upper arm. "If you gentleman will excuse us?"

"Of course," Gryder said. "It is your party, Laura."

"Yes," she said, "it is." Now she gave Carla a very pointed look. "I'll return him when I've finished with him, my dear."

Carla opened her mouth to retort, but Gryder bumped her with his arm and she remained silent.

Laura Linquist led Clint across the room, nodding to her guests along the way.

"You can meet all these people later," she told Clint. "After."

He kept himself from asking, "After what?"

SIXTEEN

Three men standing together in a corner watched as Laura Linquist led Clint across the room.

"She's got him," one of them said.

"Well, why not?" another asked. "She's going to be donating a lot of her husband's money."

The third man said, "And he won't even be aware of it. Poor Arnold."

"Hey," the first man said, "he had years of that woman servicing him. Now he's a vegetable in a wheelchair and she's in charge. I think she's earned it."

"You're right," the second man said. "Arnold was a real bastard."

"A kingmaker," the third man said, "but a bastard."

"Indeed," the other two said.

They all sipped their drinks and began to discuss the stock market.

* * *

"You know what she's up to, don't you?" Carla asked Gryder.

"Of course I do."

"And that's okay with you?"

"As long as she pays for the privilege," he said, "she can do whatever she wants."

"Clint won't go along."

"Why not?"

"Believe me," she said, "I know."

Gryder looked at her and smiled.

"He turned you down, didn't he?"

She tightened her lips.

"Wow, that's never happened to you before, has it, Carla?"

"I'm not finished."

"Well, you are for now," he pointed out, "because there he goes, with Laura."

"I repeat," she said, "he won't go along."

"I guess we'll just have to see," he told her. "Can I get you a drink?"

"How?"

"What?"

"How will we know?"

"It will all depend," he said, "on how much she donates to the cause." He took her arm. "Come on, I'll get you a drink."

"What are you going to tell the governor?" she asked as he led her away.

"Don't worry," he said, "the governor can wait."

In another part of the room Lieutenant Governor Wheeler and Walter Dixon stood off to one side, each holding a drink. They watched Laura Linquist take Clint one way, and Will Gryder tug Carla Beckett in another.

"I'm still not sure about this," Dixon said.

"Come on," Wheeler said. "Look at the attendance tonight."

"Laura's parties are always attended this well," Dixon pointed out.

"But I've been talking to people, Walter," Wheeler said. "They're fascinated by this possibility."

"The Gunsmith in Congress, representing Texas?" Dixon said.

"It's a possibility."

Dixon finished his drink and said, "I need another one."

"The whiskey is flowing freely, my friend," Wheeler said.

"It should be."

SEVENTEEN

Laura Linquist took Clint from the main ballroom of the huge house into a smaller room, lined with books on every wall.

"My husband's den," she said. "He used to spend hours in here, reading, or doing business at that desk."

The desk was cherry wood, with spindly legs. It looked very expensive to Clint. She walked to it, ran her hand over the smooth surface.

"Where is he now?" Clint asked. "I thought you were taking me to meet him."

"He's in bed upstairs," she said. "He's been in a vegetative state for months. At least, that's what the doctors tell me."

"I see," I said. "Then why bring me in here?"

She looked up at him, keeping her hand on the desk.

"I brought you in here so we could get better acquainted." She left the desk and walked toward him. "I need to see what I'm going to be investing my husband's money in."

"Well, then," Clint said, "what do you want to know?"

She crossed the room to him and stood in front of him. She was a lovely woman, despite the small lines that were forking at the corners of her mouth and eyes.

"Kiss me," she said.

"What?"

"Kiss me . . . please."

"Mrs. Linquist—"

"Laura."

"Laura, do you really think that's a good idea?"

"I do, yes," she said. "A very good idea. Do you find me unattractive?"

"I think you know you're a beautiful woman, Laura."

"And desirable?"

"Yes."

"To you?"

"Laura—"

She licked her lips and said, "I'm just asking."

"Well . . . yes."

"Then kiss me."

He hesitated, then leaned forward and kissed her on the lips.

She laughed.

"You call that a kiss?"

She wrapped her arms around his neck and kissed him fully, completely, her mouth wide open. He kissed her back in self-defense. Eventually, they each melted into it, and it went on for a while. When they finally parted, she stepped back, breathless.

"Well . . . not bad."

"I passed?" he asked.

"The first test."

"The first . . . what's the rest?"

She stepped to him again, put her hands on his chest, started to undo the buttons of his new, crisp white shirt.

"Laura—"

"Are you going to resist me?"

"Well—"

"Is it the woman?"

"The woman?"

"What's her name? Carla? She's a lovely girl. Is she yours?"

"No, no," he said, "nothing like that. She's my . . . assistant."

"I see. Let me show you something."

She stepped back, put her hands behind her back, and her gown fell away, leaving her naked from the waist up. She had very good breasts, large and firm, with heavy undersides and dark nipples.

"I try to take care of my body."

"You're lovely," he said, dry-mouthed.

"Are you interested?"

"Under normal circumstances I'd say yes."

"And why are these not normal circumstances?"

"Well, for one thing, you're married," he said. "For another, you have a house full of guests."

"There's only one guest I'm interested in," she said. "The rest can fend for themselves. As for my husband, he has always been too old to have sex with me. He is aware that I go elsewhere for it."

"But this isn't the place—"

"The time or the place? It's perfect." She stepped

closer to him. As she did, her gown fell to the floor and she stepped out of it. She was completely naked now.

"There are a lot of people in the house, making noise, which is good. Musicians playing loudly, as I instructed them to do." She leaned against him, flattening her breasts to his chest, her crotch to his, and whispered into his ear, "I'm a screamer."

She reached between them, massaged his hard cock through his trousers.

"Oh," she said, softly; "I see that you *are* interested."

EIGHTEEN

Laura kissed him while she took his penis out of his pants. She stroked it while he ran his hands down her back to her buttocks. As it grew in her hand, she became more and more interested in that part of his body.

She got down on her knees so she could use two hands on him. She pressed the burning column of flesh to her cheek, rubbing it there, then over her lips. She stuck her tongue out and used it to wet him, moaning at the same time.

"Wait," he said abruptly.

She fell back onto her haunches and remained that way, staring at him.

He removed his gun belt, set aside where it was within easy reach, then undid the belt on his trousers and dropped them to the floor.

"Oh," she said, and came back to him. With one hand she grasped his shaft, and with the other she cupped his heavy sack. Then she took him into her mouth, slowly, inch by inch, until he was fully engulfed. She began to slide him in and out of her mouth, slowly at first, then faster and faster . . .

"What do you supposed they're doing?" Carla asked Gryder.

"What do you think they're doing, Carla?" Gryder asked with a smile.

"I don't want to think about it," she said.

"Jealous?"

"Disgusted."

"Tell me," Gryder said, "why do you think Clint resisted you?"

Her lovely mouth tightened. At first she wasn't going to answer, but then she decided to.

"He's playing games with me," she said. "He wants the power."

"And does he have it?"

"Not yet."

"You're so concerned about what he's doing now," Gryder said, "I think maybe he has."

"That's ridiculous."

"Why don't you go and see what he's doing?"

"Why don't you go and get a lady another drink?"

He did, chuckling as he went.

Lieutenant Governor Wheeler looked up and saw the governor approaching him.

"Sir," he said when the man reached him.

"Wheeler," the governor said. "Where's Mr. Adams? Has he arrived?"

"I, uh, I'll have to find out for you, sir," Wheeler said. "I'll ask Will Gryder."

"Never mind," the governor said. "I'll find him and ask him myself."

"Yes, sir."

As the governor walked away, Dixon came over.

"What's wrong?"

"He's looking for Adams."

"Is he still with Laura?"

Wheeler shrugged.

Dixon rolled his eyes.

Gryder was crossing the room with Carla's drink when he ran into the governor.

"Will!"

He turned and stopped.

"Sir?"

"Is Adams here?" the governor asked. "I'm waiting to meet him."

"Uh, yes, sir, he's here."

"Why didn't you bring him to me?"

"He insisted on meeting Laura first."

"Ah."

"He said since she was the hostess, and a possible contributor . . ."

"I understand," the governor said. "He's thinking like a candidate already."

"Yes, I suppose he is."

"Very well," the man said. "When he's available, then."

"Yes, sir," Gryder said. "I'll bring him right over."

The governor nodded and walked past Gryder, presumably to go to the bar. Gryder walked over to Carla and handed her the drink.

"It's taking too long," she said.

"Yes," Gryder said, "it is."

NINETEEN

Clint allowed Laura to suck his cock for as long as he could take it, then reached down and pulled her to her feet. He kissed her mouth roughly, bruising it, then took her breasts in his hands. He lifted them to his mouth, sucked, and licked her nipples while she moaned, then he began to bite them.

"Oh Christ," she said impatiently, "I have guests to see to, Clint. Come here."

She grabbed his hard cock and pulled him toward a flimsy-looking sofa. She settled down onto it, and opened her legs to him.

"Are you sure this will hold us?" he asked.

She put her hands between her legs and said, "Goddamnit, figure it out!"

He did. He kept one foot on the ground so that both of their combined weights were not on the sofa. He guided his cock to her wet pussy and slid himself in.

"Oh, God, yes," she said, closing her eyes.

He took one of her ankles in each hand, held her spread, and began to fuck her that way.

"Yes, oh yes," she said, squeezing her breasts, rubbing them hard. "Just like that. Keep going, keep going . . . ohhhh God . . ."

He kept going, all right, decided to give her what she obviously wanted, as hard and fast as he could. He was also working off some of the sexual tension from being around Carla. Walking away from her the night before, while she was sitting on his bed, had been hard, but he couldn't let her take control that early in their relationship.

And this woman, this hungry and demanding woman, thought she was in control, too, because of her beauty and her money, but at the moment he was in charge, and by the time he got done, she'd have a hard time walking straight.

And so would he . . .

Laura Linquist strolled back into the ballroom on Clint Adams's arm sometime later, a smile plastered on her face.

"You bastard," she said. "I'm raw."

"I think you asked for it, ma'am."

"And you gave it to me."

"I did my best."

"Really?" she asked. "You mean there's no more where that came from?"

"Laura," he said, "we're at a party, remember?"

"I remember," she said. "Here comes your campaign manager."

"He probably wants to talk to you about contributing," Clint said.

"Oh, don't worry," she said, "I'll be contributing. And I'll get my friends to contribute. You're as good as elected, my friend."

"Your friends?"

"My lady friends."

Clint wondered what that meant as Will Gryder approached them.

"I've been looking for you two," he said. "The governor wants to meet you, Clint."

"I'm ready."

"And Laura, you and I have to talk."

"I'm ready, too," she promised.

"Don't disappear on me again," Gryder said to her. "I'll be right back as soon as I introduce Clint."

"I'm going to get myself a drink," Laura said, giving Clint a sly look. She licked her slightly swollen lips. "I need one."

Clint allowed Will Gryder to take him across the room toward the governor, who was talking at the moment to three other men.

"How did it go with Laura?" Gryder asked.

"It went fine."

"Is she going to contribute?"

"She says she is."

"With her on our side," Gryder said, "we should be able to get a lot of her friends to contribute."

"Her lady friends," Clint said.

"What?"

"She says she can get her lady friends to contribute."

"She's talking about wives getting their husbands to contribute," Gryder said, "and I'm all for that."

Clint was, too—unless Laura Linquist meant he'd have to do to other wives what he'd just done to her. Clint didn't know if he had the energy for that. Although it would have been very interesting go try.

"Okay, here we go," Gryder said. "Time to meet the big man himself."

TWENTY

"Governor?" Gryder said.

The governor turned, drink in hand, and looked at Gryder, then at Clint.

"Excuse me, gentlemen," he said to the other three men. "Time for me to meet the guest of honor."

The three men, no doubt local dignitaries, waited to see if they would be introduced as well. When it was plain that this was not to be the case, they moved away.

"Governor," Will Gryder said, "this is Clint Adams."

"It's a pleasure to finally meet you, Mr. Adams," the man said, extending his hand.

Clint shook hands with the politician and said, "I'm told I have you to thank for this."

"This party?" the governor said. "That's all Laura Linquist."

"I mean the campaign," Clint said, playing along with the official story. "It was your idea that I run."

"And a brilliant idea, I think," the governor said.

"Well," Clint said, "I guess that's something we're going to find out."

The governor looked at Gryder.

"Will, why don't you give me some time with Clint?" he said.

"That's fine, Governor," Gryder said. "I have to talk to Laura anyway."

"And have somebody bring Clint a drink, won't you?"

"Sure."

"Champagne," the governor said.

"I'll have Carla bring it over."

"Fine, fine," the governor said. "Lovely girl."

Gryder nodded and walked away.

"Clint," the governor said, "can I call you that?"

"Of course, sir."

"I think running you for Congress here in Texas is going to be one of the best ideas I ever had. I think you're going to prove me right."

"I hope so, Governor."

"Look at all these people," he said, taking in the room with a wave of his hand. "They're all trying to look at you without really looking. They're all looking at your gun. They've never seen a politician who wears a gun."

"I doubt they'll let me wear it in Washington, D.C., if I get there."

"Well, that's okay," the governor said. "By then you'll already be in office and it won't matter."

"I hope you're right," Clint said, even though he would have hated to be elected. In fact, he hated this party, and his boots were killing his feet.

"Ah, here comes the lovely lady with your champagne," the governor said.

Clint saw Carla approaching them with two glasses.

"Hello, Carla," the governor said.

"Governor," she said. "How nice to see you." She handed Clint a glass. "Governor?" she asked, holding the other drink out.

"No, no," the man said, "I hate champagne. You drink that one, my dear, and take Clint around to meet some of the people."

"Yes, sir, I will."

"Clint, we'll talk again."

"Thank you, sir."

They shook hands and the man strolled away.

"Are you happy?" Carla asked Clint.

"About what?"

"You know what," she said. "You disappeared with that . . . woman."

"Our hostess?" Clint asked. "She wanted to talk with me about my campaign."

"Oh, please," she said. "You expect me to believe you were talking?"

"We even talked about you."

"What?"

"She said you were a lovely girl."

Carla glared at him and said, "She did not."

"She did."

"I wonder what her tone of voice was when she said it," she said. "And I wonder what you two were doing at the time."

"Discussing my campaign."

"Fine," Carla said, "have it your way."

"She's determined to help me get elected," Clint said. "Oh, by the way, that's what you're supposed to be doing as well."

"Don't you worry about me," she said. "I'll do my job."

"Fine," Clint said. "Then let's start now. Suppose you take me around and introduce me."

He held his arm out for her to take. Reluctantly she did.

"And try to look happy doing it," he said.

TWENTY-ONE

Clint spent the rest of the evening making small talk with potential contributors to his campaign. By the end of the night his feet were throbbing, his head was aching, and he knew why he hated politicians. Most of the men he spoke to were obvious phonies and blowhards. None of them would have lasted an hour on the trail, or in a poker game.

Late in the evening Clint was standing off to the side, holding a glass of whiskey rather than another glass of champagne. He was hoping to be left alone for a while, but that didn't seem to be in the offing as a tall man in a suit and a tan hat came walking toward him, his head down. As the man approached, however, the man raised his head and Clint smiled.

"Well," he said, "as I live and breathe, Deputy Marshal Heck Thomas."

The badge on Thomas's vest caught the light in the room as Heck smiled and stuck out his hand.

"Hello, Clint. Or should I say, Congressman?"

"Please don't."

"That doesn't sound like somebody who wants to get elected."

"I don't."

Thomas frowned.

"But you're runnin', right?"

"I am," Clint said, "like I said in my telegram."

Clint had sent a telegram to Fort Smith even before he arrived in Austin. Thomas was wearing a badge for Judge Parker's court, but despite that had come in response to Clint's call for help.

"How long can you stay?" Clint asked.

"Long enough to keep you alive, I guess."

"You tell the Judge what you were doing?"

"Of course I did," Thomas said. "I told him I was trackin' a dangerous desperado into Texas."

Both men laughed.

"Come on," Clint said, "let's go to the bar and I'll get you a drink."

"You gonna fill me in on what's goin' on?" Thomas asked. "You coulda knocked me over with a feather when I heard you was runnin' for office."

"I will tell you," Clint said, "but not here. This shindig is about to break up. I'll tell you the whole story in a little while, when we get away from here."

"Good," Thomas said. "I could use a drink."

"Do you have a place to stay?" Clint asked as they approached the bar.

"No," Heck said, "I just got here."

"You'll stay with me."

"With you?"

"They've given me a house, with a lot of rooms and a great cook," Clint said.

"Sounds like an offer I can't turn down."

"Whiskey?" Clint asked as they reached the bar. "Or champagne?"

"Whiskey," Heck said. "Champagne is swill."

As Clint handed Heck his drink, Gryder and Carla came walking up.

"We've been looking for you," Gryder said.

"Well, here I am. This is my friend, Deputy Marshal Heck Thomas."

"Deputy?" Gryder asked.

"In Judge Parker's court in Fort Smith," Heck said.

"And what are you doing here, Deputy Thomas?" Carla asked.

"Right now I'm lookin' at a beautiful gal," Heck said.

"Heck, this is Carla Beckett. She's my . . . assistant. And this young fella is Will Gryder, my campaign manager."

Gryder nodded and said, "You didn't answer Carla's question, Deputy. What brings you here?"

"Keeping my friend alive, I hope," Heck said.

"I don't understand," Gryder said.

"I sent Heck a telegram and asked him to come here and watch my back during the campaign."

"Watch your back?" Gryder asked. "You expect somebody in Austin to try and kill you?"

"Will, I expect somebody to try and kill me every day of the week."

"Well . . . yes, of course, I mean . . . being who you are, I suppose . . ."

"It's only natural," Carla said.

"Yes, I suppose you're right."

"Heck will be staying at the house with me," Clint said. "In fact, we're headed there as soon as we finish these drinks."

"That's fine," Gryder said. "This shebang is just about over. But you better say good-bye to our hostess."

"Yes," Carla said, "I'm sure she'll be terribly upset if you don't."

"I'll do that right now," Clint said. "Why don't you two keep Heck company, and then we'll all go to my house for a nightcap."

As he walked away, Carla said, "Nightcap. Already he's talking like a politician."

TWENTY-TWO

Clint made sure he said good-bye to Laura Linquist while she was surrounded by a good number of her other guests. He shook her hand and looked her in the eye. She squeezed his hand and said, "We'll talk again, Mr. Adams, soon."

"Yes, we will," he agreed.

He went and found Gryder, Carla, and Heck Thomas, and they all went back to his house.

The three men who had been standing together the whole night watched as Clint approached Laura Linquist and said good-bye.

"When are we supposed to try for him?" one of them asked.

"I haven't got word yet," the leader said. "Don't worry, it'll be soon."

"Maybe they want him to get deep into the campaign first," the third man said.

"That's a possibility," the leader said.

"Who's gonna pull the trigger?" the second man asked.

"We'll see," the leader said. "It'll all be in the orders."

"He's leavin'," the second man said.

"Let him go," the leader said. "The time will come. Don't worry."

"His" house.

Clint was surprised to find himself thinking of it that way. Getting too comfortable in that house would be a mistake.

He unlocked the front door and allowed the others to enter ahead of him. Gryder turned up some of the lamps.

"Wow," Heck said, "this place is impressive."

Clint walked over to a sideboard that had been fully stocked with whiskey and brandy.

"What's your pleasure?" he asked.

"Brandy for me," Carla said.

"And me," Gryder said.

"To tell you the truth," Heck said, "I'd really like a cup of coffee."

"I don't know if Mrs. Bigelow is awake," Clint said. In fact, he didn't even know if the cook lived in or not. But as if in answer to a prayer, Mrs. Bigelow came walking into the room, fully dressed and alert.

"Sir, can I get anything for anyone?" she asked.

"Mrs. Bigelow, good evening," Clint said. "I think our guests might like some coffee."

"Of course, sir," she said. "Right away."

She turned and left the room.

"You're a miracle worker," Gryder said.

"In what way?"

"That woman," he said. "I've never seen her so . . . amenable. I think she loves you."

"I don't know about that," Clint said, "but I think I love her."

"Well then," Heck said, "if it's not too much trouble, I could use something to eat."

"That's fine," Clint said. "Carla, could you go and ask Mrs. Bigelow if she has anything she can prepare for Heck?"

"No."

"What?"

"I'm not going in her kitchen," Carla said. "She'll kill me. She doesn't love *me*."

"Okay," Clint said, "I'll do it. Carla, keep Marshal Thomas entertained."

He left the room, noticing as he went that none of the three people were speaking.

He entered the kitchen, being careful to knock first.

"Mrs. Bigelow," he said, "did we wake you when we came in?"

"No, sir," she said without elaborating on what she might have been doing. Clint could already smell the coffee brewing.

"One of my guests is Deputy Marshal Thomas," he said. "He's going to be staying with us for a while." He'd already decided what tack to take with her. "I kind of want to show you off. Do you have anything you could make for him to eat? He only just arrived in town a couple of hours ago."

"I have some leftovers I can heat up," she said. "Actually, enough for everyone."

"That's great," he said. "Heat it all up and whoever wants it can eat some."

"Yes, sir."

"Thank you, Mrs. Bigelow."

"You're very welcome, sir."

Clint thought that as long as he showed the woman respect, they'd get along just fine.

TWENTY-THREE

They ended up all sitting around the dining room table, eating some leftover stew that Mrs. Bigelow must have prepared even before Clint arrived.

"This is great!" Heck said enthusiastically. "You got yourself a helluva cook there, Clint."

"I know it."

Gryder and Carla were eating in silence, even though Clint felt his campaign manager had a lot he wanted to talk about.

Heck had brought one carpetbag of belongings with him, and it was on the floor by the front door. They were finishing up their feast when Julius, the butler, walked in.

"I'm so sorry I wasn't here when you arrived, sir—" he started, but Clint cut him off.

"That's all right, Julius," Clint said. "This is Deputy Marshal Heck Thomas. He's going to be staying with us for a while. Get him settled in a comfortable room. His bag is by the front door."

"Very good, sir."

"Hey, wait a second there, pardner," Heck said, standing up. "I'll come along with ya." He looked at Clint. "I'm kinda tired. Guess I'll see you in the mornin'."

"Okay, Heck. Good night."

He nodded and said, "Night, folks," to Carla and Gryder.

"Good night," Carla said.

Gryder just nodded.

Heck left the room with Julius. They heard them talking in the front room, Heck telling Julius he'd carry his own bag. And then they went upstairs.

"We need to talk about tonight," Gryder said.

"You could've talked in front of Heck."

"Clint, I don't even want to talk in front of Carla."

"That's my cue to leave," she said, standing up. "Gentlemen, I'll see you in the morning."

"Let me see you home, Carla," Clint said.

"That's okay," Gryder said. "There's a coach and driver waiting out front to take her."

She waggled her fingers at them and walked out. They heard the door open and close, and then the sound of a horse pulling away.

Mrs. Bigelow came out of the kitchen.

"I have to clean up."

"Can you do that later, Mrs. Bigelow?" Gryder asked.

"I cannot," she said. "Later I'll have to make breakfast. I won't have time to clean up."

"Let's go in the other room, Will," Clint said, "and let the lady clean up."

"Yeah, okay."

They stood up and walked into the living room.

"You want another brandy?" Clint asked.

"Sure."

Clint poured him one and handed it to him.

"None for you?"

"I hate that stuff. What'd you want to talk about?"

"Some of the people you met tonight."

"Like who?"

"Let's sit down and go through them."

"Okay," Clint said, "but I've got to warn you, I don't remember too many of them."

"I'll remind you of the ones you should remember," Gryder said. "Why don't we start with Laura?"

"I think I can safely say," Clint replied, "Laura's taken care of."

Gryder recited a litany of names, only a few of which Clint could remember. But when Gryder went into more detail, they began to take form in his memory.

"This is all about strategy, Clint," Gryder finished. "You've got to know who the players are."

"Yeah, okay," Clint said. "I'll keep that in mind."

"And speaking of players, tell me about this Heck Thomas."

"Nothing to tell," Clint said. "He's a deputy marshal, and he's my friend. I asked him to come watch my back."

"And you do that wherever you go?" Gryder asked. "Have somebody watch your back?"

"If I can."

"This Thomas, he'll watch his manners?"

"His manners?" Clint repeated. "I didn't ask him to come here for his manners."

"No, I guess not." Gryder had been seated on the sofa. Now he stood up. "I better be going."

"In the morning for Mrs. Bigelow's breakfast?"

"Of course. See you then."

Clint walked Gryder to the door. As he closed it behind him, he heard Heck coming down the stairs. The tread was too heavy for Julius.

"That's some butler you got," Heck said as Clint turned to face him. Heck was wearing a gun in a shoulder holster, something he'd started doing when he was a railroad detective.

"I don't know him real well."

"Well, he made sure I was comfortable and then he disappeared," Heck said. "Yet I feel like he's watchin' me."

"Maybe he is."

"I'll have that brandy now," Heck said, "and the explanation."

"Sure," Clint said. "Let's go in here."

TWENTY-FOUR

"So the whole thing's a sham?" Heck asked.

"Shh," Clint said, "Julius might still be around. Yeah, it's a sham."

"And you're just waitin' for somebody to try to kill you?"

"Right."

"You like having a target on your back?"

"No, I don't *like* it," Clint said. "But the plan seems sound to me."

"The government's plan," Heck said. "They don't care if they lose you in the process."

"Well, I hope they care."

Heck blew some air out his mouth.

"You didn't hear this from anybody you trust, did you?"

"Well . . . Jeremy Pike. I kind of trust him."

"And when's the last time you saw him?"

"It's been some years," Clint admitted.

"You call him your friend?"

"Not exactly."

"Would you trust him to watch your back?"

Clint hesitated only a moment, then said, "Yes."

Heck put his glass down and sighed.

"Okay," he said. "I'm goin' to bed."

"Me, too."

Clint took Heck's glass and set it on the sideboard, then they walked to the stairs together. Julius appeared before they went up.

"Will you be needing anything else, sir?" he asked.

"No, Julius," Clint said. "You can go to bed."

"Thank you, sir."

"Oh, Julius?"

"Yes, sir?"

"Does Mrs. Bigelow sleep on the premises?"

"Yes, sir, she has a room behind the kitchen."

"Okay, thank you."

Julius nodded, then disappeared down a hall.

"How's he do that?" Heck asked.

"What?"

"He seems to melt into the walls."

"Well, he came with the house," Clint said. "He obviously knows it real well."

"So what's the plan?" Heck asked. "I mean, the real plan."

"The real plan is for you to keep me alive, while I find out who's been killing candidates."

"You want me to keep *them* from killin' you?" Heck asked. "Or anybody?"

"Anybody along the way," Clint said. "And in the end, the people I'm looking for. Just watch my back, Heck."

"Okay," Heck said, "but first I gotta get some sleep. I'll start watchin' in the mornin'."

"Here's hoping nobody tries to kill me tonight," Clint said as Heck walked upstairs.

The three men charged with killing Clint Adams sat in the Bloody Rose Saloon, waiting for their boss. When the man walked in, he came right over to their table.

"You three," he said, "you got trouble."

"How's that?" Andy George, the leader, asked.

"Adams has help," the man said. "He brought in a friend of his, Heck Thomas."

"Thomas?" the second man, Chris Ritter, said. "Ain't he a railroad dick?"

"Used to be," George said. "Now's he's a deputy marshal working for Judge Parker."

"A marshal?" Brian Castle asked. "What's he doin' here?"

"Adams sent for him," their boss said. "So now you got two guns to worry about."

"We can take 'em," George said.

"I'm betting you can't," the man said, "so I'm telling you to hire more help."

"But—"

"I'll put up the money," the man said. "It won't come from your end."

"Fine."

"And the new men? They shouldn't know anything about me. Got it?"

"We got it."

"Let me know when you get that done."

"The job?"

"No, damnit," the boss said. "Get the help, and then let me know. I'll let you know when to do the job. It's a sensitive thing. Got it?"

"We got it."

"Don't screw this up," the man said, "or it'll be your last job."

He stalked out as the three men exchanged glances.

"Who do we get?" Castle asked.

"Right now," George said, "get three more beers, and then we'll decide."

TWENTY-FIVE

The next morning, at breakfast, Will Gryder told Clint—and Heck Thomas—what the schedule for the day would be.

"We'll be meeting with three different groups during the course of the day," he said. "One of the meetings will be over lunch, and one over supper. Carla, you'll need to take Clint to pick up his new suits. He's going to need them today."

"Right."

"New duds," Heck said, raising his eyebrows at Clint. "Nice."

"And take the marshal," Gryder said. "If he's going to be around us, he could use a couple of new suits, too."

"Hold on there," Heck said. "I can't afford—"

"It's all taken care of, Heck," Clint said. "It's on Texas."

"Well, in that case—I like blue."

"Get that done early," Gryder said to Carla, "and then bring them to the first meeting."

"Right."

"I'll see you all later."

Gryder left the table, and the house.

"When you gentlemen are ready to go shopping, I will be in the living room."

She left Clint and Heck at the table, still finishing the feast Mrs. Bigelow had laid out for them.

"Are we permitted to go armed?" Heck asked.

"They want me to, which suits me," Clint said, "and I want you to."

"Sidearm, or can I wear the shoulder rig?"

"Whatever makes you most comfortable," Clint said.

"Well," Heck said, "I wouldn't wanna ruin the lines of my new duds, but I think I'll go with the shoulder rig. I like it."

"That's fine."

"Man, this grub is good," Heck said. "I can see I'm gonna put on a few pounds before this job is done."

"Yeah, I had the same thoughts."

"Be a shame if our new clothes ended up not fitting us anymore. I'd kinda like to take mine back to Fort Smith with me."

"I'll make sure you do." Clint got up. "I'm going to get dressed."

"I'll be right up, soon as I finish this last stack," Heck said, forking some more flapjacks onto his plate.

When both men were dressed, they met Carla in the living room.

"We're ready," Clint said.

"Good. Let's go."

"My horse is in the town livery," Heck said.

"We've got a coach to take us," Carla said. "Don't worry."

"You bring your horse?" Heck asked Clint as they stepped outside.

"No, left him behind," Clint said. "I figured they'd be dragging me around."

Outside they started down the walk toward the coach when Heck saw a glint of sun off metal across the street.

"Down!" he shouted. He spread his arms and lunged, taking both Clint and Carla to the ground. The shots came, and a couple of bullets went over their heads and slammed into the front door.

"Hey—" Carla cried as she went down, but she fell silent when she heard the shots.

Clint and Heck drew their guns. Clint remained where he was, shielding Carla with his body. Heck ran across the street to see if he could catch the shooters. The coach driver had taken shelter beneath the coach.

Heck came walking back and said, "We're clear."

"Are you all right?" Clint asked Carla, helping her to her feet.

"I think so," she said. "Who was that?"

"Heck?"

"Didn't see anybody," the marshal said. "They fired and then ran."

"What was that about?" Carla asked.

Clint and Heck exchanged a glance. Heck holstered his gun, decided to let Clint handle the explanations.

"I'll go and check on the driver."

"Clint?" Carla said. "What's going on?"

"Probably just somebody who recognized me yesterday, maybe followed us back here," Clint said. "They waited for daylight to take their shot."

"They tried to kill us?"

"Me," Clint said. "They tried to kill me."

"But . . . just because of who you are?"

"Exactly."

"That is so . . . unfair."

"So's life, Carla," he said. "Do you want to go back inside?"

"No," she said, "no, let's get in the coach and get the hell away from here."

TWENTY-SIX

When they reached the store, Heck got down from the coach first, looked around, then assisted Carla down. She was followed by Clint.

"You sure you're okay?" Clint asked the driver.

"I'll be fine, sir."

"You want to come inside?"

"No, sir," the driver said. "I'll wait out here."

"Suit yourself."

In the store they took a moment to check Carla over again. She had no bruises or scrapes that they could see, and she insisted she was fine.

"Let's get those suits."

Clint's were ready. When it came to Heck's new clothes, Carla decided his didn't have to be as impeccably tailored as Clint's, so they bought him a couple of suits off the rack. He tried them on, and approved them.

"Wrap them up," Carla told the clerk.

"You've got good taste, Miss Carla," Heck said.

"It's just Carla," she said, "and thanks."

"And since you're dressin' me, ya might as well call me Heck."

"Heck," she said, "I didn't thank you for saving my life back at the house. Thank you."

"It weren't nothin'."

"How did you know those men were there?" she asked.

"I saw the sun reflectin' off the metal of their guns."

"That's remarkable," she said.

The clerk came with their packages and they went out to the coach, where the driver—true to his word—was waiting.

"Back to the house to change?" Clint asked Carla.

"No," she said, "you're dressed well enough for lunch, but we'll have to go back so you both can change for supper."

"Okay," Clint said.

"You're the boss," Heck said.

"Tell your friend that," Carla said.

Clint ignored the remark as he helped her up into the coach.

"I'm gonna ride with the driver this time," Heck said.

"Riding shotgun," Clint said. "Good idea."

Heck kept a wary eye out for trouble as they drove to the location of the lunch.

"What's this group supposed to be?"

"It's the Austin Women's League," Carla said.

"Really?"

"You'll get a lot of contributions from them if they like you."

"Them or their husbands?"

"Same thing," she said, "but yes, for the most part the money would come from their husbands." She patted his arm. "Just be your charming self."

"I'll try."

"I don't know how you'll be able to do it," she said. "To tell you the truth, I'm still shaking. I've never been shot at before."

"Well, it was me they were shooting at, but I see your point," he said. "Maybe . . ."

"Maybe what?"

"Well, maybe somebody else should be doing this job," Clint suggested.

"Oh, no," she said, shaking her head, "this is my job, and I'm going to do it."

"Well, let's go then."

Inside they found Will Gryder waiting for them.

"It's about time."

"We had some excitement," Carla said.

"Tell me about it later."

"Somebody tried to kill Clint."

"What?"

"A couple of shots," Clint said.

"Where?"

"In front of the house."

"They might have done it, too, but Marshal Thomas saved us."

"That's great," Gryder said, "but these women are waiting to hear from Clint."

"Hear from me?"

"Sure," Gryder said, "you have to give a speech."

"A speech?" Clint said. "You never told me I had to get up in front of a bunch of women and talk."

"That's what campaigning is all about, Clint," Gryder said. "Speeches."

"What am I supposed to say?"

"You'll figure it out," Gryder said. "Come on. Carla, stay with the marshal."

"Deputy," Heck said as Gryder rushed Clint away.

"Let's get a good spot," Heck said to Carla. "This I gotta see."

TWENTY-SEVEN

Everyone was surprised, especially Clint. He had the women eating out of the palm of his hand almost from the moment he started speaking. Then the women clamored to ask questions. Gryder finally had to call a halt to the proceedings. It was time for them to have lunch.

Clint found himself sitting among a bunch of women, having chicken for lunch. Gryder was seated at a different table, and Heck and Carla were at a table by themselves—from where Heck had a good view of the room, and Clint.

When the afternoon was over, they all returned to the house, where Gryder was able to see the bullets in the front door.

"Was it close?" he asked.

"The bullets went right over our heads," Carla said.

They went inside.

"Did you see who fired them?"

"No," Heck said. "I ran across the way, but they were gone already."

Gryder looked at Clint.

"This doesn't come as a surprise to you, does it, Clint?"

"Not really," Clint said. "Somebody's always taking a shot at me sooner or later."

"Okay then," Gryder said, "maybe it's a good thing we got this over with now."

"You think it's finished?" Carla asked. "If they shot at him once, they might try again."

"And they probably will," Heck said.

"And we have the marshal here to see that they miss again."

"Deputy," Heck said.

Julius came into the living room at that point and asked, "Is there anything I can do, sir?"

"No, Julius," Clint said. "We just came back to change clothes."

"Yes, sir. Shall I draw baths?"

"Baths?" Heck asked, looking at Clint.

"That's okay," Clint said. "We'll just go upstairs and change."

"Good," Gryder said. "The next meeting is at three, and then after that we have supper."

Clint and Heck went upstairs to don some of their new clothes.

They came out of their rooms at the same time, in their new suits.

"How's it fit?" Clint asked.

"Just fine." Heck shrugged his shoulders. "A little

tight in the shoulders, because of the shoulder rig. Mine's not tailored, like yours."

"Still feels like it's choking me."

"Hey, let's take a look out the windows first from up here."

"Good idea," Clint said. "We can use any of the front bedrooms. Come on."

They went into an empty room, up to the windows, and looked out.

"See that doorway?" Heck asked, pointing. "I think they fired from there."

"They would have had more luck from the roof," Clint said.

"Maybe," Heck said, "they weren't tryin' to hit you."

"You mean you? Or Carla?"

"I mean nobody," Heck said. "I was lookin' at those bullets in the door. They were a little high."

"So you think they missed us on purpose?" Clint asked. "Why would they do that?"

"I don't know," Heck said. "I guess we'll have to ask them when we find them."

"We better go down," Clint said. "Gryder will be getting nervous."

"He does seem to be a nervous kind of fella," Heck said. "I don't like him very much."

"I'm sure that fact won't bother him much," Clint said.

"And what about the girl?"

"Carla? What about her?"

They started down the hall.

"I think she likes you a little more than the job calls for."

"No," Clint said, "I think she's just doing her job."

They went downstairs, where Gryder was waiting impatiently.

"Oh, good. You're here. Carla, go out and tell the driver we're ready—"

"No!" Clint said. "She's not goin' out there alone. Not after what happened this morning."

"All right, then," Gryder said, "we'll all go, but let's move or we'll be late."

"Do I have to make a speech this time?"

"No," Gryder said, "this time you'll just have to answer some questions."

"From women?"

"No," Gryder said. "This time it will be all men."

TWENTY-EIGHT

This time Clint was asked questions by the Merchant's Association of Austin—and the questions were harder, more political.

Heck stood in the back of the room, keeping a wary eye out for anything suspicious. Carla stood next to him. Gryder was up front somewhere, among the crush of men.

"How's he doin' with this political stuff?" Heck asked.

"Don't tell him I said this," Carla replied, "but he's doing pretty well."

"Yeah?"

"His answers are pretty good, and that's even without Will Gryder's coaching."

"Is he tellin' them all what they wanna hear?" Heck asked.

"Not exactly," she said, "but he's telling them how

he feels, and that seems to be doing the trick. But as we go along, the questions are going to get harder."

"He'll handle it," Heck said. "That boy can handle anything."

After the meeting with the Merchant's Association, it was time for supper with the next group.

"Who are these people?" Clint asked.

"We're eating with some of the wealthiest couples in Austin," Gryder said. "By dessert I want you to convince them to contribute."

"I'll do my best."

Carla and Heck were already in the coach, Heck once again riding shotgun. Clint and Gryder got in the back with Carla.

"Where to?" the driver asked.

"Stockman's Steak House," Gryder said.

"Hey, that's one of the best restaurants in town!" he said.

"That's the point," Gryder said. "Not only the best restaurant in town, but the best steaks."

"Well," Clint said, "that suits me just fine."

"Me, too," Heck agreed.

When they got to Stockman's, there was a room in the back of the restaurant reserved for them. They arrived before any of the guests.

"Clint, these people are very important. You'll have to pay special attention to them all."

"I'll do my best."

"The men *and* the women," Gryder went on.

"I'll keep that in mind."

The first couple arrived, and Gryder went over to greet them.

Clint walked over to Carla.

"Would you do me a favor?"

"What kind of favor?"

"Would you stay with me during the meal?"

"Stay with you?"

"Yes, sit with me."

"But . . . why?"

"Because they're all going to be couples here," Clint said.

"Ah, you think they'll take to you more if you look like a couple, too."

"That's the idea."

She shrugged and said, "Well, sure, why not?"

"Don't mind me," Heck said. "I'll just sit by myself."

"I'd get you a girl, Heck, but you have a wife someplace, don't you?"

"As a matter of fact, I do. Don't worry about it, boy. I'll be keepin' an eye out for trouble while I work on a big, thick steak."

As more couples arrived, Gryder brought them over to meet Clint, who in turn introduced them to Carla. She got into the spirit real quick, and hung on to Clint's arm until they all sat down to eat.

The steaks were thick and juicy, the beer was cold, and all the guests were interested in what Clint thought he could do for Texas.

Once again Carla was surprised at how well Clint

fielded questions, and worked on both the husbands and the wives. From the look on Will Gryder's face, he was pleased, too.

"And what about you, my dear?" one woman asked Carla.

"What do you mean?"

"Well, when Mr. Adams gets into Congress, will you be right there with him?"

"I'm sure I will, Mrs. Adcock," Carla said to the woman. Then she added, "After all, I am his assistant."

"Is that all, my dear?" the older woman asked.

"Angela," her husband said. "Behave yourself." The man looked at Carla. "I'm sorry, my wife can sometimes be . . . incorrigible."

Carla simply turned her head, keeping a pleasant look on her face, even though Clint knew that inside she was seething.

He admired her.

TWENTY-NINE

After the last of the rich couples had left, Clint turned to Carla and said, "I wouldn't be friends with any of those people."

"Don't fool yourself," she replied. "They don't want to be friends with you either."

"Then why were they here?" he asked.

Will Gryder joined them and said, "They want to be on the winning side."

Clint, still seated, looked up at him and said, "You know, I've never asked. Who's my opponent?"

"The incumbent," Gryder said. "Congressman Turner has been in office for three terms, and expects to win a fourth. We want to disappoint him."

"Well, what's left to do today?" Clint asked.

"Nothing," Gryder said. "I'm going home from here. You can do what you want."

Heck Thomas came over to join them and said, "I'd like to get a drink."

"That sounds good to me," Clint said.

"Me, too," Carla said.

Heck looked at her.

"You ain't gonna go into a saloon."

"Why not?"

"Because a woman who looks like you in a saloon means trouble."

"I won't cause any trouble."

"Yeah, you will," Heck said. "You won't wanna, and you won't start nothin', but there'll be trouble."

"That's silly," she said.

"I'll leave you folks to your discussion," Gryder said. "I'll see you all at breakfast tomorrow at the house."

He gave them a salute, and left.

"We can get a drink here, Heck," Clint said. "Carla won't cause any trouble here. It's a restaurant."

Heck shook his head, but didn't say anything.

"Let's go," Clint said, and led the way out of the back room into the restaurant.

They got a table and told the waiter they only wanted drinks. He took their order.

When Clint and Heck had their beers and Carla a glass of brandy, she said, "See?" to Heck. "No trouble."

"Like Clint said, this ain't no saloon," Heck answered. "In a saloon there'd be trouble."

"But why?"

"Because you're too damned beautiful."

"Why, Marshal Thomas," she said, "are you flirting with me?"

"I ain't flirtin'," Heck said, "and I ain't gonna sit here and drink." He downed his entire beer and stood up.

"There's a saloon across the street. That's where I'll be until you two come out."

"What's the matter with him?" Carla asked as Heck walked out.

"He just wants to stand at a bar and have a drink," Clint said. He waved at the waiter to bring another beer.

Andy George stood at the bar with a beer, waiting for his boss to arrive. When he did, he joined his subordinate and called for a beer.

"I was surprised to hear from you so soon," the man said. "You got your help already?"

"We got 'em."

"Where are your friends?"

"Out collectin' them," George said. "We got three more men."

"Six against two?" the man asked. "Is that enough?"

"Yeah, although we're facing two good men."

"Adams has Heck Thomas backing him up," the man said, "and he's a lawman. Is that a problem?"

"For the right amount of money," the man said, "nothing is a problem."

"All right, then."

"When do we go?"

"Not for a while," the man said. "We want his campaign to get going first."

"Why?"

"It's not important that you know why," the man said. "Just follow orders."

"So what do you want us to do in the meantime?"

"Do whatever you want," the man said. "Just be available when I want you."

"One of us will always be here," George said.

"That's fine." The boss drank his beer, set his empty mug down. He took out an envelope and passed it to Andy George. "That's fine. We'll talk again soon."

As he left, George opened the envelope to see a sheaf of bills. A taste of what was to come, but it was a taste the others didn't have to know about.

He pocketed the envelope and told the bartender, "Another beer."

THIRTY

"This has not been an enjoyable day," Clint said.

"When you agreed to run," Carla asked, "did you really think it would be fun?"

"Well, no, but I didn't think I'd be making speeches, and having supper with people I didn't like—"

"Trust me," Carla said, "it's going to get worse before it gets better."

"Well, thanks."

"I'm just telling you the truth," she said, "and when you're involved in politics, you're not going to find a lot of people who will do that."

"But you will?"

"Well," she said, "you're the one who cured me of playing games."

"Yeah, what was that all about?" Clint asked.

"Wasn't it obvious?"

"Do you always jump into bed with men you just meet?" he asked.

"In the interest of telling the truth . . . no."

He picked up his beer and finished it, then sat back in his chair.

"I'm tired," he said. "I don't get this tired after spending a day in the saddle."

"Then you should probably go home and get some rest."

"And maybe you should come with me," he said. "You need some rest, too."

"Do I?"

"Well," he said, "you need some time in bed."

At the house they did not run into Mrs. Bigelow or Julius on their way in, and went right up to Clint's bedroom.

Carla seemed to get shy once they were inside. Clint wondered if it was because this was the place where he had rebuked her when she tried to seduce him.

"I feel silly now," she said, sitting on the bed as she had last time.

"Don't feel silly," he said. "I'm sorry I did that to you."

"Don't be," she said. "It taught me some humility."

He walked to the bed, took her by the upper arms, and stood her up. She tilted her chin up for a kiss and this time he didn't disappoint her. Her lips were generous and warm, her tongue a light flutter in his mouth.

The kiss deepened. When it ended, the clothes began to come off. Finally, Clint was seated on the bed while Carla pulled off his boots, and then his trousers. His gun had been set nearby, within reach.

When he was naked, his cock sprang up from between his legs, and Carla went right for it. She stroked it and licked it while he groaned and fidgeted, and then leaned forward and took it in her mouth. She sucked him avidly, moaning as she slid the length of him in and out of her mouth.

He ran his hands through her beautiful hair, which she had let down. It cascaded down her back, and he reached beneath it to touch her smooth skin. When she cupped his testicles in one hand while continuing to suck him, he felt as if he wasn't going to last much longer, so he pulled her off him, lifted her to her feet, and pushed her down on the bed.

"My turn," he said. He got on the bed with her, positioned himself between her legs so he could press his nose to her moist pussy. She gasped when he touched her with his tongue, and then he went to work on her. He licked and sucked her into a frenzy, reached up to fondle her breasts and nipples at the same time.

When she began to buck beneath him, and gush so that the bed grew wet beneath them, he slid up on her, pressed his cock to her wet portal, and slipped into her easily. He fucked her slowly at first, actually giving her time to recover her breath, but then began to increase the speed of his strokes. He slipped his hands beneath her to cup her moist buttocks, and she pressed her feet flat on the mattress so she could lift herself up each time he drove into her.

From that point they just continued to lunge at each other until Clint finally exploded inside her, during which time they both groaned and cried out loud, completely unmindful of whether or not there was anyone else in the house . . .

They lay together on one side of the bed, because the other was still soaked with her juices.

"Now I'm really mad at you," she said.

"Mad? Why?"

"Because if you hadn't resisted me, we could have had a night like this already."

"Well," he said, holding her close, "this one is far from over, don't you think?"

"Oh yes," she said, snuggling up to him, "far from over . . ."

THIRTY-ONE

The next two weeks of campaigning went like that, meetings and lunches and suppers during the day, and sex at night. Mrs. Bigelow gave Carla long frowns every morning when she came down with Clint for breakfast. Of course the woman knew Carla was spending her nights there, but she never said a word.

It was also obvious that Julius knew, but he went about his duties each day without saying a word, or casting a disapproving glance. Clint still didn't know where he went or what he did when he was off duty—if, in fact, he was ever off duty.

Heck knew what was going on, but he kept his silence, simply followed Clint during the day, and then kept watch over the house at night.

After two weeks Heck told Clint they had to talk. They went into the living room together one evening while Carla was dressing for supper, and Will Gryder had not yet arrived.

"You think this is gonna go on much longer?" Heck asked.

"The campaign?" Clint asked. "There's still weeks of it, maybe more."

"I mean, before there's another try at you," Heck said. "You've got to get back to work, right?"

"I heard from the Judge, and he ain't happy," Heck said. "And he ain't mad at me, it's you."

"Me?"

"He says it's all your fault I ain't been workin'."

"Look, Heck," Clint said, "I don't want to get you into trouble with your boss—"

"Just relax," Heck said. "I can still squeeze another week out of the ol' boy, but after that maybe you should find somebody else to back your play. Maybe Bat? Or Wyatt? Or that Jeremy Pike guy?"

"I can talk to Pike about that next week," Clint said. "I understand we're supposed to put in an appearance in Washington."

Heck made a face.

"I hate Washington."

"I know," Clint said. "I'm not so crazy about the idea either. I sort of wish these people would make their try before then."

"That would suit us both," Heck said.

Gryder arrived at that point, admitted by Julius, who informed him of where Clint and Heck were.

"Will," Clint said. "Want a drink?"

"A brandy would go down well at this point."

"What's the problem?"

"The polls," Gryder said, accepting a glass. "We're behind."

"Clint is losin'?" Heck asked.

"I know," Gryder said, "I can't believe it either." He looked at Clint. "And there's another thing."

"What's that?"

"Before we go to Washington next week," he said, "the incumbent wants to meet with you."

"What for?"

"Who knows? Maybe he wants to ask you to quit."

"But why, if he's winning?"

"It's politics, Clint," Gryder said. "Anything could happen."

"So, what do you think?" Clint asked. "Should I go and see him?"

"You almost have to," Gryder said. "It would be rude not to."

"What's this feller's name?" Heck asked.

"Turner," Gryder said, "Congressman Big Ben Turner."

"Never heard of him," Heck said.

"What kind of man is he?" Clint asked.

"Stubborn," Gryder said. "He refuses to face the fact that times are changing. That's why we have to get him out of office."

"Okay, so when do we do this?"

"I can set it up tomorrow," Gryder said. "We'll have to go to his house, though."

"Is that a problem?"

"It shouldn't be," Gryder said. "But we can bring Heck along anyway."

"I'll be there," Heck promised.

Carla came into the room, wearing a red dress that impressed all three men.

"Are we ready to eat?" she asked. "Or is there a problem?"

"I was just telling Clint that Old Turner wants to see him."

"That old lech," she said. "He pinches my bottom every time I see him."

"So smack him," Clint said.

She looked at Gryder.

"Can I do that?"

Gryder just shrugged.

THIRTY-TWO

The next morning Gryder missed breakfast, but picked up Clint, Heck, and Carla with a cab drawn by two horses that was large enough to carry all of them. In spite of that, Heck still insisted on riding in the "shotgun" position.

"Does he know how many of us are coming?" Clint asked.

"Oh yes," Gryder said. "He's always glad to see Carla, and he said he's looking forward to meeting the famous lawman, Heck Thomas."

"Well, that's fine. And what's the occasion, if there is one?"

"Ostensibly," Gryder said, "we'll be going to his house for lunch."

"But we just had breakfast."

"Well, the congressman eats breakfast at five a.m. every morning," Gryder said, "so lunch is pretty early for him."

"What time does he eat supper?" Heck asked, looking back at them.

"About two."

Heck shook his head.

They pulled up in front of a three-story mansion in a neighborhood of three-story mansions. Heck seemed amazed that there were so many of them.

"People actually own these?" he asked. "They're not hotels?"

"Hey," Gryder said, "this is the state capital after all."

They all got down from the coach and Gryder told the driver when to come back.

"How long did you give us?" Clint asked.

"I told him to come back in an hour," Gryder said. "I'm kind of hoping you'll shoot the old boy by then."

"And I *can* slap him, right?" Carla asked. "I'm just double-checking."

Nobody answered. It would be up to her to take that as a "yes."

They mounted the huge porch and Gryder knocked on the door. A butler who was in his sixties answered the door, and seemed to recognize Gryder.

"Sir, the congressman is waiting in the solarium."

Heck leaned over to Clint and asked, "The what?"

"I think it's a big room made of glass."

"This way, please."

The butler led the way, leaving it to one of them to close the door, which Gryder did.

The solarium was, indeed, a big room with glass walls, and a large, portly man was waiting there for them, wearing a silk dressing gown. If the congressman had been awake at 5 a.m., Clint wondered why he had not yet gotten dressed. And he also wondered why the dressing gown had to be yellow. The congressman looked like a big tent.

"Sir, your guests have arrived," the butler said.

"Excellent! Thank you, Lewis."

"Sir," Lewis said. "I will see to lunch."

"Yes, do that."

Gryder stepped forward and said, "Good morning, Congressman. Thank you for seeing us today."

"Hell, I wanted to meet my opponent a long time ago. Bring him on!"

"Yes, sir," Gryder said. "This is Clint Adams."

"A pleasure, sir," Turner said.

Clint stepped forward and shook the congressman's huge, pudgy hand.

"When I heard you were running against me, I was excited, positively excited."

"Really?"

"Of course. This is exciting, don't you think?"

"Well—"

"And Carla," the congressman said, cutting Clint off, "how wonderful to see you again."

"Hello, Congressman," she said, remaining where she was, across the room.

"And this must be Deputy Marshal Thomas."

Heck was still staring at the apparition in yellow, and seemed startled when the congressman spoke to him.

"Yes, sir," he said.

"Happy to meet you, Congressman," Heck said.

"I'm glad you're all here," the congressman said. "I want you all to stay here. Lewis will bring coffee out for you, or something stronger, if you like. I am going to go and dress for lunch. If you'll all excuse me?"

"Of course, Congressman," Clint said.

They were actually all glad to see the man go, and glad that he was going to change out of the yellow dressing gown. Clint was just afraid to see what the man was going to come back wearing.

The butler, Lewis, returned with coffee for them all. He offered stronger but no one took him up on it.

After he left them, Heck said, "I wouldn't wanna look at this fella Turner under the influence. Who knows what he's gonna be wearing when he comes down?"

What he was wearing was a lavender suit with a yellow shirt, and a yellow rose in his lapel.

"Well, has Lewis been taking care of y'all?" he asked.

"Yes, sir," Gryder said, "we've been well taken care of."

"Good, good," Turner said, "then let's all go in to lunch."

The congressman in his lavender suit led the way to the dining room, where they were greeted by a huge table covered with food.

The congressman invited everyone to dig in, and then proceeded to attack the table like a horse at a trough. He piled several plates high. There was a second table set up for the diners to sit at, and he went to the head of it and sat down.

As the rest of his party had eaten breakfast recently, they all took what they figured was a polite amount of food and joined him at the table.

"Mr. Adams," the congressman said, "how have you been finding our state capital? Is it to your likin'?"

"It's fine," Clint said. "It's quite a city."

"Yes, it is," Turner said. "Has the lovely Miss Carla been showin' you the sights?"

"She has," Clint said.

"Delightful," the big man said. "Delightful. And how has young Will here been at running your campaign?"

"Aces," Clint said, playing the happy candidate to the hilt. "He's doing a bang-up job."

"And yet I am still in the lead," Turner said happily.

"That's a temporary situation, Congressman," Gryder said. "I assure you."

"Ah, I like your confidence, young man," Turner said, his mouth full of fried chicken.

Clint had to admit the chicken was delicious, he just wished he wasn't still full of Mrs. Bigelow's breakfast.

The congressman kept the conversation going, asking Heck to regale them with some of his adventures as a detective and a lawman. Very little of what was discussed struck Clint as a reason for him to have been invited to the congressman's house. It wasn't until the end of the meal that the politician really steered the conversation to the campaign.

"I think," he said to Clint, "you and I should take a walk and talk about things. Whataya say, sir?"

"That'd be fine."

"Besides," Turner said, lumbering to his feet, "after a brisk walk I'll be ready to go back for seconds."

Clint didn't bother pointing out that the man had already had seconds, thirds, and fourths. He probably had his own way of counting.

THIRTY-THREE

Congressman Turner took Clint outside to walk the grounds behind the house, which was a well-cared-for garden. Clint saw where the man had gotten his yellow rose from.

"I thought it would be a good idea for you and me to have a private talk, son," Turner said, lighting up a huge cigar.

"That's fine with me, sir."

"Cigar?"

"No, thanks."

Turner puffed away, filling the garden with blue smoke.

"Son," he said, examining the glowing tip, "I think you oughtta step down. Quit the race."

Clint felt dwarfed by the man's size and girth, but he was not at all cowed by the man.

"And why would that be, sir?"

"Simple, really," Turner said. "You can't win. Quittin' would save you some embarrassment."

"Why would I be embarrassed?" Clint asked. "I would be a first-time candidate who was defeated by an incumbent. Where is the shame in that? On the other hand, I could be a first-time candidate who defeats the incumbent. At that point, who would be embarrassed?"

Turner "harumphed" around his cigar and said, "I can see young Gryder's influence there."

"He thinks I have a chance to beat you," Clint said.

"And what do you think?"

"I don't think it matters," Clint said truthfully.

"And why's that?"

"If I lose this time, I can probably win next time," Clint reasoned. "Any way you look at it, you have—at best—one more term."

Big Ben Turner stopped walking and turned to look at Clint.

"You're pretty sure of that, are ya?"

"Pretty sure," Clint said. He decided he might as well push the man, just in case he was the one behind the killings.

"You think a reputation as a man killer is enough to get you elected?"

Clint smiled at the man.

"I think my reputation is worrying you, Congressman. That's good enough for me."

Now Turner smiled.

"You're very confident," he said, "or you're very good at projecting confidence."

"Either way . . ." Clint said, and shrugged.

"Well, I'm very confident, too," the congressman

said. "I've been at this a long time, and I know every dirty trick in the book. And I ain't afraid to use them."

"Good," Clint said.

"Good?"

"Sure," he said. "If you use all the dirty tricks, I'll learn from the experience."

Turner studied Clint for a few moments, then seemed to come to some sort of a decision. He nodded, and stuck his cigar in the center of his face.

"All right," Turner said, "just remember, I warned you."

"I'll remember."

"Let's get back to the table now," he said. "I don't want my guests eating all the fried chicken while we're out here."

"Somehow," Clint said, "I don't think there's any danger that'll happen."

THIRTY-FOUR

They went back to the dining room, where Clint noticed Heck and Gryder were making a dent in the fried chicken. Carla was sitting off to one side, having another cup of coffee.

"I think we're done here," Clint said.

"No, no," Turner said, grabbing some chicken and putting it on a plate, "stay, eat. We'll talk some more."

"We've got things to do, sir," Gryder said, "as I'm sure you do."

"Campaigning," Turner said, "yes. It never ends, does it?"

"Yes, it does," Gryder said. "When someone wins."

"Ah," Turner said, "but that's simply when it starts all over again."

As Clint, Heck, Carla, and Gryder left the house, they saw the coach waiting for them out front.

"What did the old man want to talk to you about?" Gryder asked.

"He advised me to quit."

"Why?" Carla asked. "What reason did he give?"

"He said I would save myself from embarrassment."

"He's the one who'll be embarrassed when you beat him," Carla said. "He'll be the incumbent who got beat by a beginner."

"I guess that's what was bothering him," Clint said.

"Did he threaten you?" Gryder asked.

"I wouldn't say threaten," Clint said. "He did talk about dirty tricks, though."

"Yeah, he knows them all," Gryder said, "and he's not afraid to use them."

"I told him if he did, I'd just learn from it."

Gryder looked surprised.

"What a great answer," he said.

"I thought so," Clint said.

They took their positions in the coach, with Heck again up front.

"Where to?" the driver asked.

"Home," Clint said.

"The Capitol Building," Gryder said.

"What for?" Clint asked.

"We've got some meetings," Gryder said.

"More?" Clint asked.

Gryder sat back and nodded.

After his guests had left, the congressman continued to devour chicken, leaving many clean bones in his wake.

Lewis entered the room and stood by, waiting.

"What did you think of our guests, Lewis?" Turner asked.

"Impressive, sir," Lewis said, then added, "if we were in a gunfight."

"Exactly what I was thinking," Turner said, "before I met the man. Now I'm not so sure."

"Sir?"

"I think I need to see Mr. Chapman."

"Yes, sir."

Henry Chapman was the congressman's dirty tricks man. When the time came to be underhanded, nobody was better at it than Chapman.

"And bring out some more chicken breasts," Turner said.

"Yes, sir."

THIRTY-FIVE

It was a day of meetings, and talking about his plans for Texas should Clint be elected.

The next day it would be time to ride out to some towns outside of Austin.

On the way back to the house, Gryder told Clint, "We have to be at the train station at eight a.m. and we'll be on the road for about a week, hitting a different town each day."

"Each day?"

"That's right."

Heck turned in his shotgun seat and gave Clint a look. They were thinking the same thing. On the road would be a good time for somebody to try for him.

"Yeah, they call it a whistle-stop tour," Gryder explained. "You'll be addressing people from the rear platform of the train, and spending the nights in a special car."

"Will Carla be along for that?" Clint asked.

"I'll be there," Carla said. "I go where you go. That's what an assistant does."

That wasn't all an assistant did, Clint thought.

Andy George waited in the Bloody Rose Saloon for his boss to arrive. A message the day before had set up the meeting.

He stood at the bar with a beer, wondering if it was finally time for him and his partners to do the job.

As his boss entered the saloon, George ordered two more beers from the bartender, then carried them to the table the other man had sat down at.

George pushed a beer toward the man.

"How are your men?" he asked.

"Impatient."

"Well, that is about to end."

"It's time?"

The man nodded.

"Adams is starting a whistle-stop tour tomorrow," he said. "He'll be on the rails for a week, sleeping at night in a private car." The man leaned forward. "We do not want him coming back to Austin."

"How do you want it done?"

"Obviously."

"What?"

"Bloody," the man said. "As bloody as possible."

"You don't want us to make it look like an accident?"

"We don't want anything fancy. Just kill him," the man said. "Do not mess this up."

"Okay," George said. "Okay, we can do that. What about the others?"

"Heck Thomas is a deputy in Judge Parker's court,"

the man said. "Do not touch him. We don't care about any of the others."

"And the woman?"

"Do whatever you want to do with her," the man said. "You have a free hand this time, Mr. George, but don't get used t it."

"Yes, sir."

The man reached into his jacket and pulled out a thick envelope. He pushed it across the table to Andy George.

"You'll get another like this when you return," he said. "We will meet here eight days from now."

"Eight days," George said. "Got it."

The man stood up and left without having touched his beer. George pulled it back across the table to his side. He'd finish these two and then go and talk to the others.

That night Henry Chapman knocked on the door of Congressman Big Ben Turner's house. Lewis opened the door to admit him.

"He's in the solarium," he said.

Chapman nodded. He knew where the solarium was.

As he entered, he saw Turner sitting in a plush armchair, wearing a purple dressing gown.

"Ah, Henry, my boy," Turner said. "Sit, I'll have Lewis bring you a whiskey."

"Fine."

Chapman didn't see the big man move at all, but moments later the butler came in and handed him a whiskey.

"Thanks."

"I have some work for you," Turner said.

"I figured."

"It will take you on the road."

Chapman made a face.

"I hate the road."

"I know," Turner said, "and this is why I will pay you a lot of money. To make up for it."

"Fine," Chapman said. "What's the job?"

"You have, of course, heard of Clint Adams . . ."

THIRTY-SIX

Early the next morning Clint and Carla woke with their limbs entwined, still damp from the exertions of the night.

"Oh," she said, rolling away from him, their skin parting reluctantly because of the dampness. "I can use a bath."

"Better make it quick," Clint said.

"Do you think Julius will prepare it for me?" she asked.

Clint swung his feet to the floor and said, "I'll ask him."

"He's your butler," she said. "Don't you tell him what to do?"

"I'm not used to having a butler," Clint said. "I feel better asking than telling."

"You'd never be able to live as a rich man, would you?" she asked.

"Not if I had to wear yellow robes or purple suits, like Congressman Turner."

"Oh God," she said, "that would be funny."

"I noticed you managed to avoid getting your butt pinched," Clint said.

"I stayed away from him," she said, "because I knew I'd slap him if he did it."

"I would like to have seen that." Clint pulled on a pair of trousers. "I'll go and have Julius prepare a bath for you."

"What about you?" she asked, posing so that her breasts were thrust out at him. "Want to join me?"

"Like I said," he replied, "you'll have to be quick . . ."

Clint used the pitcher and basin method he was accustomed to and cleaned himself up. He knew if he'd gotten into the bathtub with Carla, they would have been late.

He was dressed when she came back into the room from her bath, covered only by a towel.

"Wait, wait," he said, "don't take that towel off 'til I'm gone, or we'll never get out of this room."

"Oops," she said, dropping the towel to the floor, "too late."

Clint fled . . .

Downstairs he found that Julius had already admitted Gryder to the house. Heck was seated at the dining room table with a cup of coffee Mrs. Bigelow had given him.

"Coffee?" Heck asked. "Mrs. Bigelow's got a big pot on."

"I'll have one," Clint said, and at that moment the

cook came out of the kitchen and handed him a cup. "Thank you, Mrs. Bigelow."

"Yes, sir."

She gave Gryder a pointed look, as if daring him to ask for a cup. He did not. She returned to the kitchen.

"Ready to go?" Gryder asked.

"I got a bag upstairs, and Carla's just about ready."

At that moment Julius came down the stairs with Clint's bag. He wondered how the butler had gotten it from the bedroom without disturbing Carla.

"Thank you, Julius."

"Sir."

Clint couldn't imagine anyone having a more efficient butler or cook.

"What's taking her so long?" Gryder asked.

"Come on, Will," Clint said. "She's a woman."

"And we still need to catch a train."

"Isn't it our train?" Clint asked. "It won't leave 'til we get there, right?"

"I still have a schedule."

"Well, your schedule is not Carla's schedule," Clint said. "Take it easy."

"Yeah, well . . . easy for you to say."

"What's got you so keyed up?"

"Oh, it's that old man."

"Turner?"

Gryder nodded.

"That funny old man in the bright-colored clothes?" Heck asked.

"That funny old man is also a brilliant politician," Gryder said. "And he wasn't kidding about knowing all the dirty tricks."

"So you're worried he'll try something?" Clint asked.

"No," Gryder said, "I know he'll try something. I'm just worried about when."

"On this trip?" Heck asked, standing and bringing his cup into the entry foyer.

"Maybe," Gryder said. "We just have to keep our eyes open."

"What am I lookin' for?" Heck asked. "You think the congressman would have somebody take a shot at Clint?"

"No, no," Gryder said, "you're thinking about this all wrong. When I talk about dirty tricks, it's got nothing to do with guns."

"Oh," Heck said, "then we're not talkin' about the same dirty."

"No, we're not," Gryder said. "Turner might do something to try and smear Clint's name, but he won't try to have him killed."

"How do you smear somebody with a reputation like Clint's?" Heck asked, and then added, "Or for that matter, mine. People already think we're killers."

"Believe me," Gryder said, "that fact only makes Clint romantic to these voters. It also makes him the type of man who will do what he has to do."

"So he's a threat to Congressman Turner," Heck said.

"Oh yeah."

"Even though he's ahead in the polls," Clint said.

"That doesn't matter," Gryder said. "What matters is who's ahead on election day."

THIRTY-SEVEN

When they reached the train yard, Clint was impressed. The special caboose reminded him of the train his friend Jim West sometimes used. The inside was broken up into two areas, one of which was for sleeping. The other area, which they were relaxing in, was a sitting room with a sofa and chairs.

"How do we eat?" Carla asked.

"The next car up has a kitchen and a dining car," Gryder said.

"This is really something," Heck said. "I think I need to turn in my badge and get a federal one."

"Judge Parker won't like that," Clint said.

"Who cares?" Heck asked. "It don't matter what he offers, it can't match this."

"Marshal," Gryder said, "you'll have to sleep up front in a passenger car."

Heck looked at the sofa.

"That'll do nicely for me," he said.

"But you can't—" Gryder started.

"If I'm gonna keep Clint alive, I'm gonna have to be close by," Heck said.

"He has a point, Will," Clint said.

"Fine," Gryder said. "The sofa is yours. I'll be in the passenger car."

He looked at Carla, who gave him a look back. They both knew where she was going to be sleeping.

"Fine," he said. "I'm going to go and tell the crew to get under way."

When Gryder was gone, Clint looked around and said, "This isn't going to be too bad."

Andy George waited for the last of his men to enter the saloon. Chris Ritter and Brian Castle were already there, each having a beer for breakfast.

"Do we know his schedule?" Ritter asked. "I mean, what stops he's gonna be makin' along the way?"

"Yeah, we know," George said.

"So where are we gonna do it?" Castle asked.

"We're gonna have to watch his first few stops, see what their routine is," George said. "Once we got that figured out, we'll hit 'em."

"What about the lawman?" Ritter asked.

"We don't kill him unless we have to."

"I don't wanna kill no deputy," Castle said. "'specially not one of Judge Parker's."

"Well, we won't," George said. "If we don't have to."

A couple of men entered, and since Ritter had recruited them, he went over to greet them, and brief them on the plan.

"What about the woman?" Castle asked.

"We'll talk about that," George said. "Let's keep that between us."

"Yeah, okay," Castle said. "She's good-lookin', though."

"Yeah, she is," George said.

Another man entered, recruited by Castle, who walked over to him.

George waited for all the men to get a beer in their hands, and then turned to address them . . .

Henry Chapman watched as Clint Adams entered the train with his team. The only one who worried him was the lawman, Heck Thomas. The manager and the girl wouldn't be a problem.

This job was a little different from the others he'd done for the congressman. The old boy must've really been worried this time, because he'd taken the shackles off Chapman.

"Do whatever you have to do," he'd been told.

He turned to mount his horse.

THIRTY-EIGHT

Their first stop, later that day, was a town called Round Rock.

"Last election Turner barely took Round Rock," Gryder explained to Clint. "So we have a good chance here."

"What do I say?" Clint asked.

"Whatever you say," Gryder answered, "say it loud, and firm."

"But . . . exactly what do I tell them?"

"You've been doing well so far," Carla said. "Just do what you've been doing, Clint."

"To tell you the truth," Clint said, "half the time I don't even know what I'm saying."

"That's okay," Will Gryder said. "Half of the people out there won't even be able to hear you. Clint, you're the Gunsmith. They just want to be able to say they saw you."

"Well . . . okay."

"Marshal," Gryder said, "I'd appreciate it if you'd

step out onto the platform with Clint, and stand just behind him."

"That's what I'll do," Heck said, "and I'm a deputy."

"Yes, fine. Carla, you just stand next to Clint and do what you've been doing."

"Which is what, to your mind, Will?" she asked.

"Stare at him adoringly."

"I've been doing more than—"

"He knows that, Carla," Clint said. "Where are you going to be, Will?"

"I'll be out in the crowd, listening to them," Gryder said. "I want to hear what the people are saying."

"And after Round Rock?"

"Georgetown, Belton, Waco, and a few others," Gryder said. "Next week we'll take the train in the other direction."

"And what's Turner doing?" Clint asked. "I don't ever hear about him going to meetings, or lunches, or making speeches."

"He's the incumbent," Gryder said. "He expects to win with just a few appearances."

"He's going to find out that's a mistake," Carla predicted.

"That's what we're hoping for," Gryder said.

The door to the car opened and a man in an apron said, "Sir? Lunch is served."

"Let's eat!" Gryder said.

After lunch Clint left Heck and Gryder in the dining room, having a discussion about something or other. He wasn't really listening. He slipped into the other car and sat down on one of the chairs to relax with his thoughts.

"Am I interrupting?" Carla asked, entering.

He turned his head and looked at her.

"No" he said, reaching a hand out to her, "come and sit with me."

She walked over and sat in the other, identical chair. She looked at the sofa.

"You think the marshal will be comfortable there?"

"Heck can sleep on rocks," Clint said. "Don't worry about him."

"I'm not," she said, reaching out to put her hand on Clint's knee. "I'm worried about you."

"Me? Why?"

"I don't think you're cut out for this, Clint."

"Campaigning?"

"That," she said, "and being a congressman."

"You mean you think I have a chance to win?"

"Well, of course," she said. "Or else I wouldn't be working to get you elected."

"But?"

"But I don't know if the job would be a good fit for you," she said. "Are you ready to leave your horse behind and exchange it for an armchair? Behind a desk?"

"I don't know," Clint said. "I guess maybe I should've given it some more thought than I did."

"Well, once you're in," she said, "it may be too late for you to get out."

"Hasn't anybody ever resigned from office?"

"Yes," she said, "but then they're never seen or heard from again. They're usually finished in politics."

"Well, I think if someone resigns from politics, they pretty much want to be finished with it."

She laughed and said, "That's a good point."

She moved her hand from his knee to his thigh, began to rub it. He could feel the heat of her hand.

"You feel tense," she said.

"Do I?"

She nodded and said, "Maybe I should relieve you. What do you think?"

He smiled and said, "I think you should lock the door."

THIRTY-NINE

Carla locked the door between them and the dining car, then came back and got to her knees in front of his chair. She rubbed her hands over both his thighs, then laid one hand on his crotch and squeezed. He was already growing hard. She leaned in, pressed her face to him, and breathed on him. The heat just made him grow harder.

Together they removed his gun belt—careful to set it within reach, even on the train—and then set about to lowering his trousers. She didn't bother with his boots, since she just wanted his pants down around his knees so she could get to his cock.

When his erect penis was pointing up at her, she fell upon it, first with her hands, and then with her hot, eager mouth. She was determined to finish him—thereby relieving any stress—quickly, before someone came along and knocked at the door.

As she sucked him, Clint lifted his butt off the chair, pushing himself even farther into her mouth. It was unclear at one point whether she was sucking his cock, or he was fucking her mouth, but it really didn't much matter.

They were both anxious to finish, figuring somebody would be along pretty soon, trying to get in, either Gryder or Heck. Her head began to bob at increased speed and he rose up to meet her, sometimes so hard she would gag. But she stayed with it, using her right hand to stroke him at the same time, and finally he gushed into her mouth with a groan . . . and the door rattled.

She backed away, wiped at the corners of her mouth, as he hastily pulled up his pants and strapped his gun back on. At that point whoever was at the door knocked.

"Get the door," he hissed at her.

Smiling, she stood up and sauntered to the door, took her time unlocking it.

Heck stepped in and looked at them quizzically.

"Am I interruptin' somethin'?"

"No," Clint said, "nothing. We were just talking."

"I'm just takin' a walk through the train, checkin' on things," Heck said. "Makin' sure we got no stowaways."

"No stowaways in here," Carla said with her hands behind her back. Clint thought the innocent look she had plastered on her face was comical.

"Okay," Heck said. "I'll just keep checkin'."

"You do that," Clint said.

Heck walked through the car and out the other door.

"That was close," Clint said.

"That was exciting," she said. "Want to do it again?"

"No!" he said. "That was supposed relieve my stress, not cause more."

Carla giggled.

Clint said, "I think we should move back to the dining car before something else happens."

"Coward," she said as they went through the door.

As had been the case so far, Clint did very well at their first three stops. Their fourth stop was to be Waco, which Gryder said was important.

"The congressman won Waco last time, but just barely. I think we can get it away from him."

"How do we do that?" Carla asked.

"Well," Gryder said, "the easiest way would be for Clint to shoot somebody."

"That's not going to happen," Clint said.

"Oh, I know that," Gryder said. "That was just wishful thinking on my part."

"Unless," Clint added, "somebody tries to shoot me."

"Well . . ."

"Don't even think about it," Carla said to Gryder.

"No, you're right," Gryder said, "we'll just have to depend on Clint winning over the crowd, and the town."

"He's been doing great so far," Carla said.

"Yes, he has," Gryder said. "Carla, why don't you and Heck take a walk so Clint and I can go over his speech."

"Deputy?" she asked. "Would you like to take a walk with me?"

"I sure would, miss," Heck said.

She slid her arm through his and they strolled away, leaving Clint and Gryder alone in the plush sitting room of the last car.

Andy George led his men into the town of Waco.

"This is gonna be the place, boys," he said. "Adams

will make his speech, and then the car will stay overnight in the train yard. That's where we're gonna make our move."

"What about the horses?" Castle asked.

"Stinnett," George said to one of the men Castle had recruited, "you're gonna stand by just outside the yard with the horses. Don't panic when you hear shootin', and don't let the horses spook."

"I gotcha."

"So what do we do 'til then?" Ritter asked.

"'Til then," George said, "we get a drink."

FORTY

Clint's speech in Waco was met with shouts of approval—but then they began shouting as soon as he stepped out onto the rear platform of the train.

Clint was not sure how many people could actually hear him, but he did as Gryder had told him—he spoke loudly and distinctly about the things they'd talked about. The people standing in the front rows were certainly able to hear him, and they screamed their approval. Others may have simply been following the leader, but at least nobody threw any fruit or vegetables at him.

Once they were done, they all went inside and Gryder said, "That went well, real well."

"Thanks," Clint said.

"Can we go out to eat?" Carla asked. "There are plenty of restaurants in Waco, aren't there?"

"There are some good ones," Gryder said.

"Suits me," Heck said. "I'll just keep my eyes peeled for trouble."

"Okay, then," Clint said. "We'd better get off the train toward the front, though, away from the crowd."

Henry Chapman drank the rest of his beer and signaled the bartender for another one. He still had a clear view through the mirror behind the bar of the men he had followed there.

There were six of them, and they seemed to have a real interest in the train Clint Adams was on. Chapman had spotted them back in Round Rock, the train's first stop. Since that time he had been following them. In Georgetown and Belton, they had watched the train and the proceedings again very carefully. They had also watched after the speech was over. Chapman was sure they were following Clint Adams and his team to get an idea of their routine.

But now, in Waco, the six men had gone directly to a saloon. This could only mean one thing. They felt they had the group's patterns down, and were going to make some kind of move tonight.

Chapman didn't like amateurs, and while these fellas may have been professional cowboys, or even outlaws, they weren't professional killers.

He felt dead sure they were going to mess this up.

Gryder took them to a steak house just off Waco's Main Street. They got a table for four toward the back, and both Clint and Heck sat so that they could observe the entire room. Business was brisk, and there seemed to be people there who had been at Clint's speech, because they obviously recognized him.

However, nobody approached them to try to talk to him, so they were able to eat in peace.

"We have a few more stops and then we'll head home," Gryder said. "So far this whistle-stop tour has gone very well."

"You sound surprised," Clint said.

"A lot about this campaign has surprised me," Gryder admitted, "but mostly you."

"Why's that?"

"Because you've done everything right," Gryder said. "Usually I'm in a position where if my candidate loses, I can blame it on him. Something stupid that he said or did. That's not the case here. If you lose, I'm going to have to admit that it was my fault. For a change, I'll have to take the blame."

"If I lose, I think we can pretty much share the blame, Will," Clint said.

"No, no," Gryder said, "that's nice of you to say, but this one's going to be on me—if we lose, I mean."

"But we won't," Carla said.

"Darn right we won't," Heck said. He lifted his beer glass. "Here's to the best damned congressman the State of Texas will ever have."

They all raised their glasses and said, "Hear, hear."

They took two small cabs back to the train yard, where the train sat, belching steam.

"I'm gonna take a turn around the yard, Clint," Heck said. "Just for a look-see."

"Wait for me, Heck," Clint said. "I don't want you to do that alone."

"Actually," Heck said, "I'm better off alone. I can melt into the dark better without you, and not be seen."

"Well, okay," Clint said, "but be careful."

"I won't be long."

Clint, Carla, and Gryder boarded the train and Gryder said he was going to the passenger car to go over some papers.

"Come on back in a couple of hours for coffee," Clint said.

"Right," Gryder said.

He went forward, while Clint and Carla went into the rear car sitting room—alone.

Andy George said to his men, "Drink up. Last one. We're gonna move."

"Now?" Castle said.

"It's dark, and they should be settled in," George said.

"But . . . how we gonna do this?"

"We talked about this, goddamnit," George said. "They ain't never gonna now what hit 'em. Just don't kill the lawman if ya don't have to."

"And the girl?" Ritter asked.

"There'll be time for the girl," George said. "And if there ain't, we make time."

He finished his beer and slammed the mug down on the table.

"Let's go!"

FORTY-ONE

Heck moved easily through the train yard, keeping to the shadows. It brought back memories of the days he'd spent as a railroad detective. He liked wearing a deputy marshal's badge better. He got to spend more time in the saddle. And being a railroad detective meant dealing with railroad men. They were the same as politicians, if not worse.

The general area looked clear. There were other trains, and other crews, but he expected to see them there. However, when he started to return to their train, he thought he saw something, and froze.

He waited there for a few minutes until he finally saw it again.

Shadows.

Moving toward Clint's train.

And then he heard a horse nickering from somewhere nearby.

He quickened his pace back to the train, hoping he'd get there in time.

Clint and Carla were sitting in the armchairs, each with a glass—she brandy, and he whiskey. She was speaking, but Clint suddenly said, "Quiet."

"What?"

"Shh," he said, and put his finger to his lips.

He put his drink down, got up, and walked to a window. Careful not to stand in full view, he peered out.

"What's going on?" she whispered.

He went back to her.

"I heard something."

"What?"

"I'm not sure. Movement."

"Could it be Heck?"

"I wouldn't hear Heck."

"Then maybe Will?"

"I don't think Will would go outside alone," he said. "He's probably still in the passenger car."

"A member of the crew, then."

"Maybe." He looked around, saw a door that he knew led to a closet. "I want you to do something for me."

"What?"

He crossed to the door and opened it. There was plenty of space.

"Get in here."

"What?"

He went to her, grabbed her arm, and led her to the closet.

"Get inside and don't come out until I come for you," he said. "Not even if you hear shots."

"Shots?"

"And I want you to stay on the floor, as low as possible."

"You're scaring me." She got down on the floor.

"And roll yourself up into a ball."

"Clint—"

He closed the door on her.

George sent three of his men to the rear of the last car, and he and Ritter went to the front. One man was watching the horses.

"Wait," he said as Ritter started to board the train. He was being too noisy.

"What's wrong?"

"Quietly," George said.

"We ain't gonna be quiet for long, are we?" Ritter asked.

"That doesn't matter," George said. "Be quiet now!"

FORTY-TWO

As Heck approached the train, he saw shadowy figures moving alongside it. He drew his gun and moved closer.

Will Gryder was reading when he thought he saw something out the window. He lowered his papers and stared out, but couldn't see anything. The lights from inside were reflecting off the glass. He bordered his eyes with his hands so he could see outside, but nothing appeared to be moving.

He went back to his paperwork.

Carla started to sweat, not only from the warmth inside the closet, but from the fear she was feeling. She tried to wrap herself up into as small a ball as possible, and listened intently.

It was quiet.

Too quiet.

* * *

Clint looked around the car, trying to find cover. There was none. If he hid behind the sofa, he'd be safe from one side, but not the other. He decided to turn the two armchairs to face each other, then crouched down between them.

And waited.

Castle led two men onto the rear platform of the train. Carefully, he turned the doorknob and opened the door. It didn't make a sound. They slipped inside, found themselves in a room with a large bed.

"Where are they?" one man asked.

"Further on," Castle said. "Just be quiet."

Castle drew his gun, and the other two men did the same. They began to move through the car.

Will Gryder grew nervous, set his papers aside, and stood up. Instead of pacing, he decided to go back and see what Clint Adams was up to. Besides, he needed a drink.

George led the way onto the train, stopped just in front of the door to the car. He put his ear to the door and listened.

"Hear anythin'?" the other man asked.

"Quiet!" George hissed.

At the moment the door to the adjoining car opened and Will Gryder appeared. When he saw the two armed men, he said, "What the hell—"

George turned quickly and hit him in the face with the butt of his gun. Gryder flew back into the car and slumped to the floor.

"Damn it!" George swore. He turned to the door, opened it, and rushed in.

Clint heard the noise outside the door and saw it open. Two men came running in, guns in their hands. Clint had never seen them before, but didn't have time to dwell on that.

They began to fire as soon as they saw him. Their bullets slammed into the back of the stuffed armchair.

Clint fired.

Heck saw the two men climb onto the car, and he raced forward. He was in time to see them strike Will Gryder and then burst into the car. As he climbed aboard, he heard the volley of shots from inside. He rushed in with his gun in his hand.

Clint held his fire as Heck Thomas charged into the car.

"Whoa!" Heck said.

"You're a little late."

"I saw shadows outside," Heck said. He looked down at the two dead men on the floor. "I think there are more."

"Three more," Castle said.

Clint and Heck froze. They saw that they were covered by three guns.

"You fellas are in a jam," Castle said. "Drop your guns."

Clint and Heck released their guns, which dropped to their feet.

Castle was unsure about what to do. The orders were not to kill the lawman, but if they killed Adams right in front of him . . .

At that moment a voice from behind them said, "Now you three are covered."

Castle turned, saw a single man standing with a gun.

"One man against three?" Castle asked.

"The way I see it," the new man said, "it's three against three."

Castle and the two men looked around nervously. Clint could tell what was about to happen, and dove for his gun, followed by Heck.

The room became filled with gun smoke and flying lead, and then was quiet . . .

Five men lay dead on the floor.

Clint looked at the man who had come in behind the three.

"Thanks, friend."

"Don't mention it. I've been followin' these jaspers for a while. There's another one waitin' just outside the yard, with horses."

"I guess we better go and get him."

"No hurry," Henry Chapman said. "He ain't goin' anywhere."

"Where's Carla?" Heck asked.

"She's in the closet—" Clint looked over and saw a couple of holes in the door. "Carla!"

He ran to the door and opened it. Carla was curled up into a ball on the floor. She looked up at him and asked, "Is it over?"

FORTY-THREE

"It's not over," Clint said.

They were back at his house in Austin. After dealing with the law in Waco, and getting Will Gryder's broken nose looked at, they simply turned the train around and headed back.

Now it was the second morning after the shooting. Gryder's nose was bandaged but he was still plowing through one of Mrs. Bigelow's breakfasts.

Heck was sitting across the table from Clint. Carla was at Clint's right.

"What's not over?" Heck asked. "We got all six of them."

"But we don't know who they were working for."

"Can't the law ask the sixth man?" Heck asked.

"He doesn't know," Clint said. "According to him, only Andy George knew, and he caught my first bullet."

"I don't understand," Will Gryder said, sounding as

if his nose was stuffed up—which it was, with cotton. "What are you talking about?"

Clint looked at Gryder. He hadn't yet told him what he was really doing running for Congress. But he had sent a telegram to Washington the previous afternoon for Jeremy Pike, requesting permission to open up about it.

"I'll tell you all about it later, Will," Clint said. "Right now we just have to keep going the way we've been."

"We missed some of our stops," Gryder said, "but we're set to go west this time."

"I don't know about that," Clint said.

"The answer might be here in town," Heck said.

"The answer to what?" Gryder asked.

"Yes," Carla said, "to what?"

Clint looked at them both, was about to answer when they heard a knock at the door.

"Who could that be?" Carla wondered.

"Julius will get it," Clint said.

Julius did get it, and brought a man into the dining room.

"Mr. Pike, sir," he said.

Clint looked up, saw the Secret Service agent standing there.

"Jeremy," Clint said, "just in time for breakfast."

"Looks good," Pike said, "but can we talk?"

"Sure." Clint took his napkin from his lap and dropped it on the table. "Follow me."

He led Pike to the living room, where they'd be alone, out of earshot of the others.

"What's going on?" Clint asked. "You come to pull me out?"

"Not quite," Jeremy said.

"Then what are you doing here?"

"I was nearby when your telegram was relayed to me," Pike said. "So I thought I'd stop by."

"And?"

"See if you were okay."

"I'm fine," Clint said. "Five men aren't. And there's a sixth, but he doesn't know anything."

"Maybe I should talk to him," Pike said, "since I'm here."

"Jeremy, I want to tell Gryder what's going on. I think the campaign has run its course for me."

"Not until we find the leader," Pike said. "Without him, they can start all over again."

"We're supposed to go on another whistle-stop tour in the next few days," Clint said. "Maybe they can put together another crew by then."

"All right," Pike said. "Give me a few more days, Clint. Meanwhile, I'll go and talk to the sixth man. Maybe he can tell me something we can use."

"What about breakfast?"

"Maybe lunch?" Pike asked.

"Sure," Clint said. "Come on back. You wouldn't believe the cook they gave me."

FORTY-FOUR

Back at the breakfast table Will Gryder announced, "I've got to go and see my doctor. I'll be back later with our revised schedule."

"Be careful," Carla said.

Gryder froze, half out of his seat.

"You think someone is going to come after me?"

"No," Clint said, "it's pretty clear they were after me, Will. You go ahead."

Slowly, almost reluctantly, Gryder went to the front door and out.

"What do we do?" Heck asked.

Clint looked around.

"What's wrong?" Carla asked.

Clint spoke to Heck.

"You ever notice that Julius is never around, but always around?"

"I know what you mean," Heck said.

"Well, I don't," Carla complained. "What's going on?"

"Are you thinkin' what I'm thinkin'?" Heck asked Clint.

"I'm thinking we should find our butler and talk to him," Clint said.

"He's supposed to have a room in the back," Heck said. "I ain't never been back there."

"Neither have I. Let's have a look."

"Clint, what's goin—"

"Just stay here, Carla," Clint said. "I'll explain when we get back."

"But—"

Clint and Heck left the dining room, found a hallway that led to the back of the house. They tried a few doors before they found the right one.

"This looks like it," Heck said.

They stepped inside. They knew it was Julius's room because there was an extra suit hanging on a frame. The room was as neat as a pin, the bed made, not a speck of dust.

"What better place for someone to be positioned than inside the house?" Clint asked. "He knows everything."

"Are you thinking he works for them, or he's the leader?"

"Well," Clint said, opening a drawer and looking inside, "I was thinking he was working for them, but what if he is the leader? The brains?"

"How did he get this job?" Heck asked.

"And why's he so good at it?" Clint asked.

At that moment the door opened and Julius walked in. He stopped halfway, his hand on the doorknob.

"Sir?"

"Julius," Clint said. "Just the man we're looking for."

"I don't understand," Julius said. "This is my room."

"We know."

"No one comes into my room," Julius said, "ever!"

"Well, we're sorry, Julius," Clint said, "and if we're wrong, we'll apologize again."

"But if we're right . . ." Heck said.

"Right about what?" Julius asked. "I don't understand."

"How long have you been a butler, Julius?"

"Many years. I came here from England, where my family was always in service."

That explained the proper way he spoke. Not really a British accent because it had probably worn away over the years.

"Julius," Clint said, "you don't have a gun in your room, do you?"

"A gun, sir?" the butler asked. "Why would I need a gun? See here, this is very improper."

Clint and Heck exchanged a glance. If Julius was lying, he was very good at it. He seemed genuinely puzzled and disturbed to find them in his room.

"Maybe we've been mistaken," Clint said.

"Yeah, maybe," Heck said.

"I believe you have," Julius said, coming into the room and leaving the door open. "Now if you would please leave, I shall have to clean this room all over again."

Clint looked around. He and Heck hadn't disturbed a thing.

"All right, then," Clint said. "We'll let you get to it."

They left the room and closed the door behind them.

"If that man's a liar," Heck said, "he's the best I've ever seen."

They went back to the dining room. The table was still covered with plates and food, but Carla was gone.

"Now where could she have gone?" Clint wondered.

"Maybe upstairs to change?"

"Her curiosity was up," Clint said. "Do you think she'd leave before satisfying it?"

"I'll go upstairs and look," Heck said. "You check down here."

"All right, good idea."

Heck left the dining room and Clint heard him going up the stairs. He decided to go into the kitchen to see if Mrs. Bigelow knew where Carla was.

As he opened the door, the first thing he saw was Carla, standing against a counter. Her eyes were wide with fright as she saw him.

The next thing he saw was Mrs. Bigelow, standing across from her.

The third thing he saw was the gun in her hand.

FORTY-FIVE

"Mrs. Bigelow?"

"Call me Lucy, hon," the woman said. "Come on in."

Clint stepped all the way into the kitchen, letting the swinging door close.

"What's going on?" Clint asked.

"I think you know, lad," the cook said.

It took him a moment, because it was so unbelievable.

"You?"

"Me."

"What's going on?" Carla asked, her voice trembling. "Somebody please tell me."

"Apparently," Clint said, "Mrs. Bigelow here works with a group who has been killing political candidates."

"What?" Carla asked in disbelief.

"Not working for, hon," Lucy Bigelow said.

"Wait a minute," Clint said. "You're the brains?"

"Now you've got it."

"But . . . why?" Carla asked.

"Politicians are ruining this country, dearie," she said. "We're just trying to give it a chance again."

"By committing murder?"

"We're making a point," she said.

"And now what?" Carla asked.

"Now another candidate dies, along with his pretty assistant." She looked at Clint. "Drop your gun belt."

"If I do that, you'll kill me."

"So?"

"I have a better chance trying to draw and fire before you can do that."

"You can't do that."

"Sure I can," Clint said. "You know my reputation."

He saw doubt creep onto her face. Maybe she was sorry she had come out from behind her facade.

"She could get killed," she said, indicating Carla.

"You're going to kill her, too, anyway," Clint said. "No, I'm going to take my chances, Lucy, so you better get ready to pull the trigger—although I don't think you'll make it."

The woman bit her lips and fidgeted in place, then suddenly threw the gun down and raised her hands.

"All right, all right!" she snapped. "Don't shoot."

"Kick the gun across the room, please."

She did as she was told, and Carla heaved a sigh of relief.

"Will you please tell me what's going on?" she asked.

"I will in a minute," Clint said. "I just have one question for Mrs. Bigelow."

"What's that?" the woman asked.

"If you were out to kill me, why not just poison my food?"

"Ruin my food like that?" the woman cried, aghast.

"You have a point," Clint replied, chuckling. "And I thank you for the fine meals."

Now that he could finally drop out of the race, he realized he'd miss having a cook.

But this one wouldn't be making meals where she was going.

Watch for

THE THOUSAND-MILE CHASE

375th novel in the exciting GUNSMITH series
from Jove

Coming in March!